MW00980225

Space Pickle

Robin Sun

SUGAR BEACH
ENTERTAINMENT

SPACE PICKLE

Copyright © 2017 Robin Sun

According to FEDERAL LAW, if you should illegally copy, download, or reproduce this book you will be subject to five years of physical labor naked in the Sun. Plus the other stuff they do to you. So you need the consent of the publisher, except for short excerpts.The characters are creations of, and owned by, the author. Reproduction of them in any form is illegal and punishable by law.

Artwork by the author

Visit the author website: robinsun.ca

ISBN 978-0-9952328-0-8 (Paperback)
ISBN 978-0-9952328-1-5 (eBook)

Printed and bound in the USA.

A big cheer for computer whiz Steve Samson, who helped get it all rolling and never took a nickel. Computer gurus Gabrielle Dumas and Rolfe Welker. Paul Darling, who bravely critiqued this and other virgin manuscripts. I've said it before and I'll say it again, Paul, you're a darling. All the great people at Sugar Beach. And eBook aficionado Jill Ronsley. Thanks to y'all!

REPORTER 'I'm speaking with Robin Rooster, the 17-year-old, uh . . . hero of the spaceship that got lost'

ROBIN 'Hiya'

REPORTER 'Tell me Robin, what happened, your engines broke down?'

ROBIN 'Yeah, and we got hijacked by aliens'

REPORTER 'Aliens! What did they look like?'

'Yeller ones, with big heads'

'WOW! How did the whole thing happen?'

'You're payin me for this, right?'

'You bet'

'OK. I'll give ya the *real* inside story. It started in a park in the city. I'd left m'home in the hillbilly hills, figurin on findin a good payin job so's I could build a sailboat.

Then float over the high seas seekin adventures and hot chicks and stuff

So I sat under a big oak called Sadie researchin a book on sailboat constructin, when a white dot across the park caught m'eye. I headed to a bench, where a newspaper sat folded

Cruised up and down the columns when all of a sudden a light blasted on in m'brain, and I stared at a headline, OFPM SEEKS SPACECREW, and let me unfold the clippin here . . . .
OK, it said

> A world survival organization called OFPM, the Organization For the Preservation of Man, is plannin a spaceflight, a socolog'cal experiment to the Moon and ^{Hic} back, exscuse, and seekin six everyday folk to see how they react to space travel and all. The ^{Hic} exscuse, dang soda I'm drinkin fizzes . . . the organization plans to evacuate our planet to bubble-top towns and cities in space aboard ships the size'a ocean ^{Hic} liners

I put the paper down, headed uptown, and got accepted

REPORTER 'How did the spaceflight go?'

ROBIN 'Great. Met this chick. Hot!'

REPORTER 'You were good, of course'

''Course. A good stud'

'Robin!'

'We had lots'a crazy conversations round the supper table'

'The ship had artificial gravity?'

'Yeah. There was seven of us, 'cludin m'skunk, Flower Butt. Sandy's the 17-year-old blonde hot chick. Heather's 28, Francis, 'bout the same age, gay as a goose. Bors a slob scientist from the Yugoslobic area, had one humdinger accent, 47. Wilbur was the Afro-Merican cap'n of the ship. I brought my BOOK'A FANTASTIC FACTS I'd read quotes from. One day round the supper table in the glass-enclosed kitchen, with stars floatin outside, I asked . . .

'In Roman times the life 'spectancy was guess A, 29, B, 49, C, hunderd 9?'

'49' said Sandy

'Wrong'

'Tree thousand' went Bors

'And the answer is . . . ' said Wilbur, who waved his hand to me

'First one — 29'

'Wow!' said Sandy. I looked in the book, and asked

'Nineteen hunderd, life 'spectancy was A, 29, B, 49, C, three thousand?'

'Has to be 49' answered Heather

'Righto' I said

'And now the life expectancy is?' asked Francis 'I know this, stupids, males — first — 70, 75, 85?'

Sandy raised her hand. Francis pointed

'The blonde one. Yes, you'
'85'
'Wrong' I said
'Tree thousand' went Bors
'I think it's 75' said Wilbur
'Correcto' answered Francis 'Ladies live to A, 49, B, 80, C, 900?'
'I think it's 900' I said 'No . . . can't be'
'Leaves 49 and 80' said Francis
'Duh . . . .' went Sandy
'Wrong'
'80' said Heather
'You're so smart'
   I looked in m'Facts book
'Says in ancient Rome, weddin guests wished a bride good luck by breakin the cake over her head'
'Good practice' said Bors
'Be kind of messy' added Heather. I shrugged and read
'Men found guilty'a rape had their test'cles crushed b'tween two stones as a punishment'
'That makes sense' said Sandy
'We should revive that custom' added Heather
'Y-E-E-O-W!' went Francis. I looked in the book
'Says doormice drizzled with honey was a fav'rite food'a the Romans'
'Why drizzled?' asked Francis
   I shrugged

'Love doormice. Eat all time. Mit ketchup though' said
Bors
'I prefer mine on a stick lightly roasted in a fire. Like
shiskabops' said Francis
'Sure' said Sandy
    We sat a second. Heather asked
'What shall we do with our evening aboard Spaceship
Faithful . . . gang?'
'How about a Roman orgy?' asked Francis
'A –– ' started Wilbur
'Wouldn't that be wild, up here in space?'
    We looked at Francis
'Just a thought. HA HA HA HA'
'Haw Haw B-U-U-R-P' went Bors
'See, Boris liked the idea'
'Yaw, HEE HEE, B-E-L-C-H'
    We had lots'a conversations like that
REPORTER 'Wacky'
ROBIN 'Yeah'
REPORTER 'How did it all begin? I mean, how did you
get chosen?'
ROBIN 'Well . . . as I said, I left the park and headed
uptown to the buildin where the ocean map company
was. Hopped the steps and looked at the index in the
lobby — noticed OFPM was in the buildin too
'Hmm' I went 'Coincidence'
    I stood at the el'vator beside a feller, 'bout 27, in a
tan suit, white shirt and orange tie, named Bill, who

asked

'Applying for the flight, are you?'

'The flight?'

'Boy, must'a been a hundred applicants this morning. Your name's . . . ?'

'Robin, Robin Rooster'

'Ha . . . Ha' he replied. The door slid open, and 'nother feller stood there a few years older in a tan suit and orange tie, havin a big mustache named Jack

'Have someone'd like to meet you Jack, this is ROBIN Ha . . . Robin HA HA . . . . Robin HA HA HA . . . Rooster, sniffle who wants to sign up for the spaceflight'

'Spaceflight? No, I'm goin to the -- ' I started sayin, but Jack grabbed m'hand and shaked it ' . . . to the map company'

'Pleased to meet you, Robin' said Jack 'See you at the meeting, Bill, three sharp'

'You bet, HA . . . HA . . . HA . . . '

'Care to join me for coffee, Robin?' Jack asked

'Could do with some apples juice'

'Swell'

'HA HA HA-CHOOO . . . Exscuse. Nobody kiss me' Bill said 'I have a cold'

'Dream on, loverboy' said Jack

'That include French kisses?' I asked

'OH!' Bill's eyes glowed 'A Hot one!'

All of us grinned, Jack put his hand on m'shoulder as we headed to the rest'runt. He asked all sorts'a questions, then back up to the OFPM fifth floor. We passed a smilin reception lady havin curly hair and a orange tie, then into Jack's office who asked more probin questions and filled forms. He said

'There's no pay involved, but bonuses if all goes OK. And you'll have one swell time'

'Great!'

'Since you're 17, we'll need a written OK from your parents'

'They can't write'

'Never learned?'

   I pointed up

'You're an orphan?'

'Was raised by m'unca Dickie'

'Dickie Rooster?'

'His name's Ostrich'

'Oh'

   Soon doctors started testin

'Tell me Robin' asked one MD, holdin this thang to m'chest 'Do you have any unusual symptoms, pains, dizziness?'

'Naw, but I think I might be pregnant'

   The doctor laughed. Bopped m'knee with a small silver hammer, kickin m'foot up. Did same with other knee, but I was ready this time — I kicked up real high horsin 'bout, accidentally bashed m'foot into a tray with silver utensils

'WOOAH!' I went, tried to catch 'em with the doc, both

us laughin

I got a part time job paintin boats b'tween rowin m'rented red dinghy round the bay, and one day Jack asked me into his office, sayin he'd a few items to bounce about. Both of us sat with our foots on the desk, mine bare as usual. Jack twirled the edges'a his big mustache

'I treat my mustache like a fine lady, Robin. Stroke, twirl her, wax her, maybe get a little rough if she won't stay in place'

'Ha Ha'

Jack aimed straight to the point as usual

'Although my handlebar isn't the only reason I asked you in today'

'Fire 'way, Lumpy' bein Jack's nickname

'OK — you're ON. YOU'RE AN ASTRONAUT!'

'I AM?!'

'YOU SURE ARE! YOU MADE IT!'

I hopped up and batted Jack on the shoulder, both of us shook hands wildly. I hopped about the room — dropped solid all of a sudden, stood lookin in the blue eyes'a the sweetest thang I ever saw — long blonde hair flowin onto her shoulders, a few freckles speckled on her nose white as snow, rosey round hips who stood 'side a OFPM lady with black curly hair and a orange tie. We smiled, and the chick moved 'long

'That's Sandra Sidewalk, Robin, the other teenager

chosen for the spaceflight'

M'jaw dropped. Jack snapped his fingers in front'a m'eyes

'Watch where you walk now, because you're very valuable property. OK Mister ASTRONUT?'

'Oh sure Jack' I replied dreamy 'I think your mustache is *beautiful*'

I walked t'ward the door, banged in the wall, then floated out

The followin weeks I was perpared for the space voyage, then flew south with Flower Butt, m'skunk. Sat b'side a perty OFPM lady who had red curly hair and white shirt, a orange tie. The small plane landed on a square orange rocket launch pad on the beach between the rollin blue sea and OFPM buildin, surrounded by swayin palms trees

The chaperone lady innerduced me to people in the buildin, and nothin excitin happened the next two weeks, except the occasional lay on the beach. They wanted us to be new to space travel, so's just a little trainin. One thang was excitin though, the meetin the crew had b'fore blastin away

The OFPM people figured it would be good for us to come together one time, so's they arranged a meetin where the six'a the crew stood in a room with Jack who flew from up north. Sandy was textin on her cell phone

'Folks, say hello to your fellow space travellers' said Jack. Sandy kept textin. Jack cleared his throat, looked to her. She throwed a kiss to the cell phone

'Hi Robin, I'm Heather Green' said a 'tractive lady, 28, with curly brown hair and green smilin eyes, who was the soc'ologist for the flight. I told her 'bout the boat I was set to build

'Hiya Robin, I'm the ship's captain' said m'next chattin pardner

'Oh Hi'

He slapped me on the back. A tall Afro-Merican feller called Wilbur, 30, with a good build. He chewed on a unlit cobs pipe, in a purple polos shirt. Who I told all 'bout the places I'd sailed

After I stood lookin in the eyes'a Sandy, the chick I'd seen up north. We started chattin excited. I told her 'bout everywhere I'd been round the world sailin m'boat. This feller across the room kept givin me the eye who I looked away to. Guess who?

Wilbur checked out Heather's butt — she looked round and Wilbur shot his eyes away

'Folks, let's change partners' said Jack. Lookin back to Sandy I stepped away and bounced into a big belly

'Hi, Boris' he said with one thick accent holdin out his hand 'I'm scientist'

Bors Bulldog was his name, 47, with a gold tooth, coke-bottle glasses, in a brown sloppy suit didn't fit so hot, brown wiry hair filled with dandruffs and some on his shoulders, others floatin in his coffee cup he didn't mind sippin away, smokin a smelly ci-gar. He had a awful odor to his breath. The feller laughed one time and I swirved aside to avoid, bashin into a stand-up ashtray, splatterin butts over the orange carpet. Everyone laughed, and helped me pick'em up

After Jack clapped hands, bein signal to change pardners, and Francis aimed toward me who stretched out his hand, twinkled his eyes as I inched back into the corner. He was sportin a yeller checkered shirt and lemon yeller scarf, tight orange shorts

'Hi, Robin, I'm Francis, your computer specialist'

'Oh . . . hiya'

'Isn't this the coolest?'

'Yeah . . . sure is'

'I'm certain we'll have one AWESOME SPACEFLIGHT'

'Oh yeah, super awesome'

Then he sparkled his eyes real deep as I pushed back into the corner, twirled m'fingers nervous-like round the window curtains. Who I told all 'bout the places I'd sailed round the planet. Francis said it sounded so *heavenly* who sparkled his eyes s'more, I pulled on the curtains nervous, which come crashin on top of us, settin the room roarin and Jack clappin. The door opened which I rocketed to, into the hall where our six chaperone ladies stood smilin in orange ties, curly hair and freckles, who whisked us away

Next day, in the dorm'tory, a knock come on the door. I opened and there was a smilin Francis

'Hi Robin'

'Oh hi, computer dude. We ain't s'posed to be social-izin, ya know, b'fore the flight. Want us to be strangers

'Little visit won't hurt. OK if I come in?'

He was already in

'Oh, NO, No . . . OK'

I hopped on the bed — and tossed nuts to m'skunk who caught'em in his mouth. Francis sat on m'bed. I hopped up and started pacin, Flower Butt follered the whole time

'Cute skunk. You bringing him on the spaceflight?'

'Yeah'

'What's his name?'

'Flower Butt'

'Nice' Francis chuckled 'Does he stink?'

'Had him fixed'

'Oh'

Francis looked round

'Lovely picture. Is that your mother?'

'Was, yeah'

'Oh?'

'Yeah'

He patted the bed

'C'mon tiger, sit, sit. You're making me nervous, pacing like that'

I sat — far away

'We should have such a FUN time'

'Can't wait'

   Jack poked his head in the door, he said

'You two aren't supposed to be socializing'

'Oh, I just wanted to ask Robin a question'

'What?'

'His . . . . . Sun sign'

'C'mon, Francis. Can't break the rules already'

   Jack led Francis out, who smiled, waved

'See you Robin'

   I nodded. Jack gave me a com'cal grin

The day we blasted off rolled round, the six of the crew, carryin OFPM flight bags and me with Flower Butt, headed to a room filled with people wearin orange ties. I spotted Sandy and Heather who come through the door — all of us waved, with Bors and Francis after, then Wilbur

The glass doors opened on the other side'a the room, and let in one DEAFENIN roar as all heads swirved about, starin to a towerin white rocketship with three orange stripes, in center of the launch pad. The doors closed and we continued fiddlin nervous with our flight bag handles, smilin wild. People patted our backs, offerin encouragements

'It's a great day for mankind!' some feller said

'You're a hero!' s'claimed a lady, pattin m'back

M'eyelid flickered wildly. The glass doors opened, 'sposed a white carpet racin to the towerin rocket that hummed in center'a the orange launch pad. People in front'a us moved aside and the six'a the crew peered through the entrance — none of us movin, Sandy started to hiccup. We felt hands nudgin our backs forward — we slowly started t'ward the door, took deep breaths, then out into the sunshine, the skunk follerin me. A ROAR 'rupted from a crowd seated in bleachers on right'a the buildin, with press people all about. We waved, smiled wild and started 'cross the carpet t'ward the waitin ship

Palms trees swayed lazly in the background as we come to half way. I was carryin the skunk. ALL A SUDDEN SIX YELLER-GREEN four foot guys, havin hair shootin out'a the tops'a their big heads and foots, appeared out'a nowheres round us. We looked to each other with eyeballs poppin — then raced full-speed t'ward the waitin rocket, the yeller fellers chasin us

At the ship two OFPM workers, one Afro-Merican and a white dude, in white overalls was bangin the button panel on the el'vator. The door opened — everyone dashed in

The yeller critters stopped, jabbered to each other, then raced out'a view

We stood with mouths open
'What the hell was that?' stammered Wilbur

'G-G-G-Got me!' said the white dude

'Looked like –– ' I started

'Aliens' continued Sandy

We all gulped

'Wasn't on the menu' said the Afro dude

He banged the button panel — the el'vator lowered

'HEY, WE'S GOIN DOWN'

The other feller hit the panel three times with his fist. A soft bell ringed and elevator started risin as we heard a female voice say

'First floor, ladies lingerie, sleepwear, bedding'

All of us looked at each other curious, the voice said

'Second floor, men's wear, shoe department'

The white feller 'splained

'We got the elevator second hand, a real bargain'

'From a department store' added the other guy

'Oh' we nodded, heard

'Third floor, hardware, sporting goods. Fourth floor, furniture. Fifth floor' A bell rings and 'OFPM SPACE CRAFT'

One'a the workers smiled to us, winked. We headed out the elevator, cross a catwalk to the hummin rocket's open oval door. All the crew stepped sideways onto the right wall which was the floor, everythin bein upside over caus'a the spaceship havin artificial gravity

We stood in a little room with benches, then on into another where six white spacesuits hanged on the walls, then through a oval door into the hallway. A glowin orange carpet raced up to the Sun at top'a the hall, which lit everythin ablaze. The engines hummed behind a door on left end'a the hall

We passed open bedrooms on both sides, glass walls on left and kitchen b'hind, the bathroom across. All of us stood on top of a few steps overlookin the head control room aglow from the Sun. A sem-eye circle row'a white seats was behind the front glass wall, the seats padded thick like bucket chairs, b'hind a curvin counter which had dials and screens buzzin and beepin. The windows in front curved up to the ceilin bein glass too, with blue and white waves rollin in on the other side and palms trees swayin. White seperators was between the windows where a voice countin numbers come out, who continued countin lower and lower. We all climbed down the steps, set our bags round a rubber plant in center'a the orange carpet. Flower Butt follered. A white piano sat to the right'a the steps. Everthang was arranged homey with pot plants b'low the windows and orange poco dot curtains

Jack smiled to us from screens on the counter in front'a the seats

'What was that, Jack?' asked Wilbur

'These yeller fellers –– ' I started sayin. Jack cut in

'Nothing! We're informed it was nothing'

'Vat mean noting?' asked Bors

'Just some prank. Kids playing a prank. Forget all about it'

'Some prank' says Sandy

'Say, great ship, ain't she? Like the polka dot curtains?'

So we 'splored round the rocket. After gathered in the control room as a guy's voice come over the speakers, sayin

'The spaceship's so solid, throw an empty pop can at the wall it's liable to cave in'

'Pop can or the wall?' asked 'nother voice

'Both'

The fellers laughed. All'a us stood with eyes wide. Someone else said

'Hey you guys . . . you're voices are being picked up on the mike'

'Sorry'

'What was that?' I asked

'Nothing' said Jack 'Some cleaners joking around'

'Positions, everyone' 'nother voice said

We sat in our white bucket chairs. The 'rangement was Heather on far left, follered by Bors, Francis the computer flit, then Wilbur the cap'n who had glowin dials and screens beepin in front, with a drifwood color steerin wheel b'fore him. Next was me and Sandy. We fidgeted in our seats and talked to Jack and other mission control fellers. Francis asked

'Isn't this EXCITING, Robin?'

'Yeah, sure is. Some scenery, huh Sandy?'

'It's *awesome*'

'This is the most THRILLING DAY of my life. Your's too Robin?' asked Francis

'Oh ya, lookit all the glowin buttons, Sandy'

The voice said a hunderd as we buckled solid in our seats, the rockets revved hearin sixty, fifty, all of us grinned round excited — forty and thirty, everyone clutched our seat handles, beads'a persp'ration rolled down our red faces; hearin twenty, fifteen . . . seven with the six of us stone solid like statues starin forward hearin five, four, one thundrous roar blasted from the engines and spaceship shaked, it inched up slowly off the launch pad, dust and smoke rised round the windows — we felt our bodies drilled back in the seats, our hands clutched tight with smoke all around the windows and the spaceship continued to rise slow. Cheerin come out the winder sep'rators as we shot higher and faster, the sky outside turned dark blue then purple, stars sparkled all round with the white Moon in front, plus Sun as we flew faster. The crew looked round to one other's bloodshot eyes and grinned. Sandy started to hiccup fierce. Francis rolled his eyeballs round his head settin everyone roarin as we relaxed a bit, tugged at our soaked wet shirt collars, peered about at the stars and overhead. Wilbur gripped the steerer, twirled her round and the rocket went clippin over the planet b'low. Then he flicked off

the engines for cruisin in orbit to check out the space-
ship. He hopped up and said
'Well! I'm heading to the bathroom'
'I already went!' said Francis. All of us laughed. He
pointed
'See that big light out there, Robin? That's Uranus'
'How can my anus be out there?'
'Old joke' said Heather. The gang roared

Well everthang tested OK as we soared over wispy
clouds and em'rald blue oceans, green continents and
white-capped mountain ranges. The sky in front come
darker, leavin a orange strip on the horizon b'hind as
we coasted to the night side. The oceans and rivers
below was all lit up silver from the stars and Moon,
cities sparkled through clouds that floated about. A
strip'a blue at the horizon in front come wider and
brighter. There was a rosy glow as golden yeller shot
across the horizon and Sun popped up red, settin all
ablaze. Long shadows from hills, mountains and
clouds stretched out in eerie-like patterns for hunderds'a miles. Everyone looked round excited as we
shot over green rollin hills and desserts'a gold

Wilbur fired the engines, pulled up, up on the
steerer as the rocket aimed t'ward the round white
Moon in front. We coasted faster and faster out'a the
planet's gravity grip, shootin into the inner depths'a
space

After the crew 'splored the ship s'more, then gathered in the kitchen for supper, with Heather chosen first cook — all of us had turns later. The kitchen was 'ranged homey with plants like the rest'a the rocket — a sideboard and sinks, a yeller fridg'rator, the walls and ceilin bein glass. A oval kitchen table rose up from the floor, with six seats round it. 'Rangement was Wilbur on far left end, who could look over the control counter in the room b'low. Heather left'a him, then Francis who chose the spot across me, Bors the far right and Sandy m'left

'Oh Heather, you're a culinary genius, an epicurean's delight' said Francis

'Why, thank you, Francis'

'Mighty fine' added Wilbur

'Thanks Captain'

'It's Wilbur'

'BurP Lofely Hedder, Hee Hee'

'Thank you, Boris'

'Yaw, Hee Hee B-E-L-C-H'

Bors swished his knife and fork round his plate sloppy, splashin on the table. One time he let fly a swish, splatterin Francis on the nose and earlobe

'B-O-R-I-S!' s'claimed Francis

'Yaw?'

'Lookit what you did!'

'Oh, sorry' Bors continued eatin sloppy

'Pass the cream please, Robin' said Francis

'Oh . . .' I passed the pitcher

'Thank you'

Francis sat across from me sparklin his eyes twirlin his spoon round his cup

'Sugar, Sandy' I said, though I don't take none

I looked up, Francis was still stairin as I scooped spoon after spoon into m'cup

'You're skunk's so cute' said Sandy 'C'mere, Flower Butt'

The skunk waddled over who she petted. I passed back the sugar

'Had him fixed so's he can't stink, but he can be unfixed'

'In case you let him go, into the wild?' asked Heather

'Yeah. Skunks can hit a target fifteen foot away' I said

'No kidding' she said

'Yeah. Know why so many skunks is hit on the road?'

'Why?' went Sandy

'Cause they ain't afraid'a nothin. Just flick their tails up at a car and BAM — they're stew'

'Speaking of stew, Heather sure can whip up a batch, can't she?' asked Wilbur

'Sure can. This is forkin good'

Francis held up a chunk'a food on his fork

'It's a culinary term — means the food on my fork is good. It's forkin good'

'BUR-R-R-P, yaw, Hee-hee'

'So you're a sociologist, Heather?' Sandy asked

'Yup. Taking notes on the proceedings'

'Well-I, we'll have to be on our best behaviour' said Francis

   SPLAT, Bors swished his knife and fork, splattered Francis again

'Son of a bitch!'

   Bors looked up

'Sorry'

'You sound like it'

   Heather placed a steamin pie on the table. Bors grabbed a slice, slomped it on his plate havin stew and gravy. Mushed everthin together with his fork, poured on katsup and dove in who we staired at

'Anyone notice how our planet is quickly receding to the rear, Robin?' asked Francis

'Oh, ya, comin smaller too'

'Is it ever!' he sparkled his eyes

'Passa cream please, Sandy' I said, though I don't take none either

'Yes' he said 'I certainly must commend them on the Absolutely E x q u i s i t e -- '

'BU-R-R-R-P'

' . . . taste they have, I mean for the spaceship'

   Francis twirled his spoon, sparkled eyes at me

'Sugar, Sandy'

   I started to scoop s'more, said

'Sure is a beautiful ship'

'Yaw'

'Beautiful women too' went Wilbur, who smiled round. Heather looked at him and Wilbur shot his eyes out the window. I said

'This pie is *real* forkin good'

'Our ship is a miniature of how they imagine the evacuation ones will be' said Heather

'Like giant Noah's Arks' I added

'How do they imagine the evacuation ships to look like?' asked Francis, who kept starin at me

'This ship is a miniature' answered Heather

'Oh'

'I'm not clear on some things' said Sandy 'They're going to evacuate the whole planet?'

'Livestock and all' answered Wilbur

'Who started OFPM?' she asked

'Some of the greatest minds on the planet'

'It's a private organization' added Heather 'Volunteers, private funding'

'So we're the first in a series of test flights?' asked Sandy

'Right' said Heather 'To see how strangers who haven't been in space will react'

'A wild, spacey vacation' 'sclaimed Francis

'And ve do some hexperiments Belch'

'We're s'posed to be a cross-section'a the popalation, huh?' I said

'I'm the token . . . Chinaman' went Wilbur

'Chinaman, huh?' asked Heather

'I'm the token . . . good-looking model type' added
Francis
'Who! Where!' I went
   Francis throwed a roll at me. Punched m'shoulder
'I heard most astronauts have seen a UFO' said Wilbur
'UFOs can leave me alone, thank you' s'claimed
Francis
'What would they want?' asked Sandy 'If they came
around'
'Maybe . . . no' started Heather
'What?' asked Sandy
'Maybe to take control'
'Like pirates' I added
'Who knows'
'I don't believe in UFOs' said Francis
'What about those things on the launch pad?' asked
Sandy
'That was kids playing a prank'

   All'a us cleared the kitchen after. I headed to Sandy's
room on right of mine, and knocked. She opened
'Sandy, uh, what're you doin tonight?' I leaned suave-
like on the door edge
'I have letters to write'
'Letters?! How ya gon' mail 'em?'
'When we get back'
   M'hand slipped and I went flyin into the room.
Sandy cracked up

'Look, we got some time. Whata'ya say . . . like to take a shower?'

Sandy just stared

'OK, kiddin. I'm next door. Just knock after your letters' I smiled, Sandy nodded 'See ya'

'Bye'

She closed the door

Headed back to m'room. Sat on the bed and stared up at the stars. The room had a glass wall which curved up to the ceilin bein glass too; with white and orange poco dots curtains at the edges'a the wall and ceilin, a orange carpet and rubber plant. Flower Butt's cage was in the corner

I opened my Book'a Fantastic Facts — a knock come on the door. Francis entered — I shot up, bopped m'head off the book shelf above

'OUCH!'

'Watch yourself there, tiger. OK if I come in?'

He was already in

'OH NO, NO, I mean . . . Hi'

'What a lovely room. Alright if I sit?'

Francis motioned to the bed

'No, No . . . I mean, no problem'

He sat

'How old are you, 17?'

I nodded

'Lovely'

Nobody said nothin

'This is all so . . . EXCITING'

'YAWNH!' I went

'So what shall we do with our evening together, tiger?'

   I yawned huge

'My! Sleepy, are you?'

'Oh yeah, Y-A-W-N-H'

'I'm sure we all are. It has been one *exhausting* day' he yawned 'OK if I smoke?'

'Why, are ya on fire?'

   Francis stopped, then chuckled

'A comedy sense. I love that'

'Oh!'

   He lit up

'SAY! Let's try our new spacesuits. We can stroll around with them on. Sound fun, Robin?'

'Y-A-W-N-H . . . If ya really wanna know, Sandy's comin over'

'Is she?'

'Yeah' I nodded

'That's OK' Francis sucked on his cancer stick 'Tell you what, have a little nap, then we'll try on our space-suits. And then Sandy *can come over*'

'Well . . . '

   He rose

'I'll turn off the light. Sleep tight. See you in twenty minutes tiger'

'Oh sure, sure Y-A-W-N-H'

'Bye bye'

'Bye Bye'

Francis flicked off the light, closed the door as I bolted up and locked it solid, then laid back fallin stone asleep

I got up for a whiz later. Opened the door, and froze. Standin there was Francis with a smile on his face. The lights was dim b'hind him
'Oh hi Robin, OK if I come in?'
'NO . . . NO . . . Gotta . . . . Whiz'
I raced by
'Oh . . . see you later'
I headed in the bathroom, and waited a long time. Poked m'head out the door, dashed to m'room — looked in the closet, under the bed, it was clear. I locked the door solid

After a knock come on the door. I didn't answer

Wilbur and Francis sat in their control room seats later, Wilbur chatted with someone and Francis to Jack on his monitor in front. Wilbur told me how it went
'I heard you've been chasing Robin' said Jack
'No sir!'
'Not what I heard'
'Stupid rumor, untrue'
'How's everything else going?'

'Boris seems to be a . . . '

'A . . . ?'

'Geek?'

'He's from a foreign country'

'Has sloppy manners. Bad breath. Dandruff falling into his food'

'We've all got differences, Francis. We're the same underneath. He's a good guy. Be friends'

'Yessir'

'No chasing Robin'

'Never!'

'Why don't you get some sleep, Wilbur's on duty tonight'

'Aye Aye sir'

Next mornin I clicked on the lamp but nothin happened. Crawled out'a bed, stumbled over a sneaker and bashed into the wall. Poked m'head into the hall — all was dark, 'cept for a 'mergency light and candles flickerin in the control room

I headed up the hall

Francis sat on the carpet b'low the control counter surrounded by parts and wires, who informed me that the night b'fore, with Wilbur on watchin duty, a POOF 'rupted out the engines room and smoke come from under the door, sparks shot from the control counter, the lights went out plus contact with mission control. Wilbur and him and Bors'd worked ever since, who got the fridg'rater goin

Sandy come round in 'jamees who I 'citedly informed all the happenins. After I headed in the bathroom and had a shower by starshine. The light come on, which I flicked off, and continued with the stars

In the kitchen later, I had a bowl'a oats. Francis poked his head in
'I've been working half the night. I'm totally drained'
he started to sing

'Hi ho, Hi ho, it's off to bed I go

Coming Robin? . . . Ha ha'
'OH! Ha ha'

Sandy and me sat in our control seats after side by side and watched stars flyin by, spottin some shootin with us pointin. Flower Butt sat on the counter who I'd toss a nut to, the skunk catchin it in his mouth
'Let me try one'
''K'
I handed Sandy a nut she tossed high and Flower Butt jumped up and caught it, munchin. Sandy laughed
'Francis is chasing you, isn't he?'
'Wants to tickle my pickle'
Sandy laughed and said
'I think he likes you'

'YEAH! Well I don't like him'

'You mean you're not gay?'

I looked at Sandy

'Ha Ha Ha . . . You a lesbo?'

'I . . . don't think so'

''Side from that, this trip is a blast'

'Can't wait to land on the Moon'

'It'll be awesome'

'Here comes Francis'

I dove under the counter

'Have you seen Robin, Sandy?' he asked

'Uh-um' Sandy shook her head

'His skunk's here'

'I'm looking after it'

'So where's the Robster?'

Sandy shrugged. I stayed crouched — Francis left

Well Francis fixed supper fancy that day, candles flickered and classic music played soft, a table cloth was loaded with orange roses, havin plates the same which he brought special. First we had soup

'What's this, Francis?' asked Sandy

'Ox tail soup, with yucca balls'

'Whose balls?' I asked

'Mine'

'I don't vant'

'Yucca balls, stupid'

Bors glared at Francis. After we ate filet chops and

scarguts, then toasted our wine glasses

'Supper is Clink lovely, Chef Francois' said Heather

'Mais merci'

'I'll have to get your Clink Clink recipe'

'Love your plates' said Wilbur

'Ha ha'

'B-U-R-R-P'

'Boris likes them'

'Yaw, Hee hee'

   I looked in m'book and said

'Very tall buildins lean toward the course of the Sun, just like plants' Lookin up, I said 'They follow the Sun's course'

'This true?' asked Wilbur

'Yup'

'Wild' went Heather

'Yeah' I read 'A pig's orgasm lasts for 'leven minutes'

'Vow!'

'Mine lasts an hour sometime' said Francis

'Sure' Sandy said

'Jealous?'

'Of you . . . ! Hah!' said Bors

'Talking 'bout pigs –– 'started Francis

'OK now' cut in Wilbur

'Accordin to a survey, over ten percent of 'Mericans have picked someone else's nose' I read

'That's a great fact' s'claimed Wilbur

'Yeah'

Francis took the book

'Look at this. In the 12 hundreds European noblemen openly displayed their *genitals* through a hole in the crotch of their tights'

'Exciting' said Heather

'Let's bring back the custom' added Wilbur

'Let's try here on ship' said Bors

'Maybe later' I added

'Sure you will' said Heather 'Say gang, how about movies tonight?'

'Great idea' went Wilbur

'B-U-R-P, Hee Hee'

'That's what I was going to say' said Francis

'Hey, who's for electing Heather our social director?' asked Wilbur

'I'm flattered'

Wilbur swung his head round to the windows like he saw somthn. He stared, then looked forward. Banged the edge'a his hand on his head three times

'Huh?' asked Heather

'Banging the pieces back in place'

'Oh'

All of us gathered in the control room and watched a pull-up screen in middle. Heather rose

'Folks, as social director, my first official duty will be . . .'

She flapped a small plastic bag filled with green tobacca

'Vas dat, dvrugs?' asked Bors, who sat with his foots in a bucket'a water and pants rolled up, smokin a smelly ci-gar

'Only a little hoochee-coo skunky tobacco, Boris. Smuggled it on board' she chuckled

'Naughty tobacco' added Francis, noddin. Heather rolled a joint

'Banana'

'Vat, banana dvrugs?'

'Papers' she said

'Bah!'

Bors rised, fetched a six pack'a beer he slugged as Heather lit the joint and passed her round. Francis took a big drag. He said extra squeaky

'This sure ain't Marlboro lights'

Then Wilbur hauled on the joint and squeaked out

'Or Salem menthols'

Francis took n'other hit, goin

'WHEE-HEE!'

Everyone come stoned, 'cludin Bors who refused total, but was breathin the smoke anyhows, Ha ha

After awhile'a watchin cartoons Francis hollered

'MUNCHEES!'

He raced to the kitchen, follered by everyone. We flipped open doors gobblin junk. Bors sprayed whip cream into his mouth, follered by little bakin candies in small plastic bottles. Then he fired more whip cream in

After in the control room we lay spread flat on our chairs, and stared up to stars, listenin to colypsos music. Then everyone drifted to bed, leavin me on night duty. I splashed cold water on m'face, sipped herbs tea and read. Nothin 'citin happened except maybe Sandy goin to the john who we waved, and maybe the visit I had from Francis in the wee hours of mornin

I was sleepily watchin the stars in the control room, hearin footsteps over the stairs. Whirled round and there was Francis approachin in orange and white striped pajamas. That dude wouldn't back off nohow. I had m'hands full

'Feeling sleepy, are you Robin?' he asked

'Oh , I'm OK' I yawned

'Mind if I join?'

'No, No . . . . OK'

Francis sat in Sandy's seat beside me

'See any flying saucer races?'

'Flyin saucers?'

'YES. There go a couple!' he pointed and touched m'arm

'WHERE?'

'Over there'

'WHERE?'

Though I didn't see any

'Ho Ho, only teasin ya fellow'

'Oh!'

He punched me soft on the arm

'Notice the stars don't twinkle up here, but just shine . . . SOLID'

'Yeah'

'Know how come?'

'No, how come?'

'It's because of the different atmosphere, than on our planet'

'Oh'

'SO, you must be feeling the tingles by now?'

'Tingles?'

'You know, pins and needles, from not sleeping'

'OH, those, yeah a bit' I yawned again

'I know something which works *wonders* for the tingles'

'Cold water?'

'Nope'

'Tea?'

'No silly'

'Joggin?'

'A massage. From someone who knows how to apply one. Feel like a massage Robin?'

'A . . . . NO . . . No thanks'

'C'mon. It'll have you feeling *simply* LUSCIOUS in seconds'

'Don't want no massage'

'You need it. Yawning like you are! You're on night watch — our safety's in your hands. C'mon, spread your chair flat and I'll . . . '

I jumped up, and moved back. Francis popped up too

'Don't be so silly. OK, maybe you'd prefer it on the carpet instead. Yes, over here, lay on the carpet'

Francis pointed to the floor. I moved back'a the seat, clutchin it

'I ain't gay, OK?'

'OK. You're being so infantile'

'Buzz off. Don't want no massage'

'Stop being so impossible! Our lives are in your hands. Lie on the carpet!'

He approached, wiggled his fingers. I moved to the next chair

'You're not afraid of me, are you?'

'HAH! ME? 'Fraid? . . . . HAH!'

'So come over here then'

'NO'

'COME HERE ROBIN'

'F-off!'

'I SAID TO LIE HERE ON THE CARPET, ROBIN!'

I stayed clutchin the chair

'DID YOU HEAR ME!'

'NO. Go 'way'

'You're being so childish. What am I ever going to do with you!'

Francis threw up his hands, exposin his hairy belly

'Well if you're going to be that way, I'm off to bed'

'OK'

'If you change your mind, you know where I can be found'

'Oh, for sure'

'Bye bye'

'Yeah, bye bye'

He headed up the stairs as I stayed starin forward. Wilbur releived me 'ventually so I headed for m'room passin Francis' door feelin the tingles all over, and fell stone asleep

Followin mornin I headed into the kitchen. The Moon was bigger through the glass walls in front'a the ship — lookin golden, with craters seen clear, rock mountain ranges and dark canyons. All'a us sat round the table. I poured a bowl'a cereal — looked in m'book
'Says the average teen girl has seven pairs'a jeans'
'How many do you have, Sandy?' asked Heather
    Sandy thought 'Six . . . maybe eight'
'I'll bet seven' said Francis
'See . . . she's average' said Wilbur
    Sandy shrugged
'Not average-lookin' I says. Everyone looked at me. I hid b'hind the cereal box, face gettin' redder
'How am I not average-looking?' asked Sandy, pinchin m'leg

43

'Ow! . . . . 'Cause you're . . . better'n average'

'I agree' nodded Francis

'Yaw, Sunday real good-looking' said Bors

'If she's good-looking on Sunday, how is she any other day?' asked Francis

'Vat?'

Francis waved his hand. I glanced at Sandy, who did same — I quickly looked away

Sandy started slicin at the chops block on the table, with a cucumber and other veges around. Heather and Wilbur was at the sideboard doin dishes

I stretched and yawned wide. Sandy shoved the cucumber into m'mouth. M'eyes bulged. I looked at Sandy who bolted up and raced to the door she held open with her foot, clutchin the glass hall wall around the door. I hopped up and chased as Sandy raced up the hall squealin 'way. I cornered her and started ticklin

Wilbur told us that after Heather pinched him big in the butt. Wilbur's eyes bulged as gigglin Heather run to the door and stood as Sandy stood, a foot holdin it open and hands clutchin the glass. Wilbur give a false charge and Heather run squealin 'way

Later in the control room I pushed a button and a big white tels'cope rose up from the counter between Sandy and me, both of us in charge'a collectin asternomic info on the trip. I scoped — Sandy jotted notes

After we headed to the kitchen for supper, with Sandy chosen chef for the day — who fixed us some super veg'tarian chow. Contact with control center was still broke

'We'll get it for sure' said Wilbur 'I know we will'

'Bet we can get by without 'em' I added

'I have one more trick up my sleeve' said Francis

'Good' added Sandy. I held up m'Fantastic Facts book

'Ten animals have been in space — now Flower Butt's the 'leventh'

'What are they?' Sandy asked

'A cow' I read — looked up 'Only kiddin — for real — a dog, bullfrog, fish, a cat, a rat, chimp, a turtle, bee, a cricket and worm'

'Wow!' went Francis

'And Francees — tvelve'

Francis throwed a olive at Bors

'Says here in the sixteenth century, it was the custom for guys to greet female visitors by fondlin their boobs'

'Hey, I like that custom' 'sclaimed Bors

'I do it all the time' I said

'Sure' said Heather

'A tribe in Africa, Australian dudes too, when guys meet, they shake each other's dorks sayin hello'

'No they don't' Sandy elbowed me

'Ooph! True . . . look'

'Pass the book please, Robin'

I passed it to Francis

'Here it is — the Alpine banana slug . . .'

'He eats lots bananas?' I asked

'Sure . . . he's only six inches long, and his PENIS is, OHMIGAWD!' Francis gasped 'THIRTY-TWO INCHES'

He clutched his chest. I asked

'That hard or soft?'

Francis looked in the book

'Doesn't say'

'If it's thirty two inch soft, must be a good SIXTY inch hard'

'Has to be soft'

'This for real?' asked Wilbur

'That's what it says . . . *WAH!*'

Six yeller-lime aliens stood on the other side'a the glass kitchen wall. We all jumped up

They was four foot high, big heads 'n round bellies wearin surfer shorts. Havin tufts'a blond hair shootin out'a the top'a their bald heads, and out top'a their foots, with three toes and fingers. Big eyes. We stared at each other

Flower Butt stamped his foots and hissed. Raised his tail high and aimed it at 'em. The alien's eyes popped — they all stepped back, like they was 'fraid'a the skunk

They chattered and pointed. I picked up Flower Butt — their eyes bulged wider — they moved back with mouths open

M'eyebrows raised
I held the skunk higher and out t'ward'em
They all bolted back
'What? Who . . . ' stammered Sandy
   I stepped forward holdin the skunk outstretched.
The aliens darted backward — up the hall, flied into
the spacesuits room and slammed the door

   After we all was in the control room, I said
'They was afraid'a the skunk'
'Are you sure?' asked Sandy
'I'm sure. That's what scared'em'
'Hope they don't come back' said Heather
'Strange-lookin critters' said Francis
'Don't believe UFOs, huh Francees?'
'They left the spaceship door open' said Wilbur, lookin
at his monitor 'Can you close it, Francis?'
'Sure'
   On Francis's screen we watched the external ship
door swung closed. Then I asked
'How come they was wearin surfer shorts?'
'Maybe they surf on their planet' s'ggested Sandy
'I bet they stole them from a ship they pirated' added
Heather
'Who would bring a pile'a surf shorts on a spaceship?'
I asked
'Surfer astronauts' said Sandy

'Wilbur, is there such a thing as surfer astronauts?' I asked
'Never heard of it'
'How about ballet dancer astronauts?' asked Francis
'OK — let's concentrate'
'If we could only get contact with mission control going' said Heather
'C'mere Flower Butt'

M'skunk waddled over who Sandy picked up — speakin cuddly to his nose
'Our super hero!'
'We're going to have to do something' 'sclaimed Wilbur
'Keep the skunk around' said Sandy

After Heather took a tray'a cookies out'a the oven — her bag'a pot was on the counter beside. She baked these cookies that just wasn't like ordinary cookies
'Have a cookie, Boris' she offered a plate of 'em to Bors in the control room, where Wilbur stood lookin at papers. Bors took a couple and bit in
'O-om good' he nodded
'Have another'

He took a couple again. Heather looked at Wilbur and chuckled

Then Bors sat with his foots on the counter, starin amazed at the stars
'Vow!'

'How about if we have a sing-along tonight?' asked Heather

'What about the aliens?' asked Sandy as she munched a cookie. Flower Butt sat in m'lap, us munchin a cookie also. I said

'I got Flower Butt. We're pertected'

'Well . . . ' went Francis

'Great idea! Good for morale. You've come through again, Heather' said Wilbur

'I brought my flute' said Sandy

'I can bat on pots' I added

'B-U-R-R-P'

'Boris will burp' said Francis

After all of us piled into the control room. Francis piddled at the piano on left'a the stairs. The rest'a us spread round on cushions on the orange carpet. I sat b'low the glass kitchen wall and batted on pot bottoms. Sandy tooted her bamboos flute by my side. Heather strummed a l'il gui-tar. Wilbur held a couple'a soup spoons bowl to bowl in one hand, and rippled them off his spread fingers, bounced them from his knee makin a clickety-clak. Bors stayed in his seat clippin his toe nails and smokin a ci-gar. Flower Butt stretched out in m'bucket seat watchin as we broke into song after not so smooth song, lookin in sing-along books which was supplied

'Play polka' said Bors

'Don't have none. OK, number thirty-one, I've Got

Rhythm Inside' said Francis, our m.c. We flipped through our books
'I'll sing lead, y'all sing choruses and la-las'
   Francis sung solo while plunkin the piano

Plunk Plunk

'I was once so lonely   bored, my life was only

a chore till you came up the street   You gave me a glance

my heart began to dance

and suddenly life was so sweet

You sent me a smile that said my life was new
I looked in your eyes and knew you felt it too

I was once so lonely   but those days are only

shadows of a time gone by

   Now I've got'

'rhythm inside'

                                                sang Sandy

'I've got rhythm inside'   and Heather

             'I've got rhythm inside'

                                I sang

'I've got rhythm inside'
'I've got rhythm inside'

                     went Bors 'n Wilbur

Francis horsed round at the piano, twitched his butt at us. We all laughed and clapped, havin right pig fun

Next song Heather popped a string. She went to her room and returned with a bottle'a cracklin rosey we passed round, follered by a joint. Bors refused total on the joint, watchin ever scornful as it went by. He got up and fetched a six-pack, and all'a us come corked again

After awhile Sandy tickled m'ribs 'cause I'm real ticklish. I bolted up, Sandy stretched her fingers like lobster's claws click-clickin chasin me up the stairs and long the hall, both of us tore into Sandy's room at the end'a the hall — I grabbed a piller and flung it b'hind, caught Sandy on the nose as she come through the door. She crinkled her face, then let out a roar and tore after me click-clickin away, got me on the bed where I lay gigglin

I rose and closed the door after a bit, lay 'side Sandy placin a kiss on her lips and both of us kissin hotter. I started strokin Sandy's neck suave-like, lickin a bit and unbuttonin the top of her blouse, both of us kissin hot. ALL OF A SUDDEN THE BLOODY DOOR BURSTED OPEN, the light come on and *Francis* stomped by the bed, who stood with his back to us while lookin out the window

'◯KAY everyone, ◯KAY now, enough of that. We're running a clean ship, BREAK IT UP. It's Friday evening . . . time for FUN. Wonderful fun fun fun fun fun fun fun'

Sandy and me untangled and looked at Francis

'◯Kay now. Everyone up and at'em. Party time. Let's all have a slurp in the control room'

'FRANCIS!'

'Yes Robin'

'Dude, you intruded' said Sandy

'Did I? Wel-l-l, can't have a party alone, nosir. There I was all by myself in the control room . . . '

'*Francis!*'

'Yes Robin?'

'Leave please'

'No, I won't. Not until we have a slurp together. Why it's Friday evening, time for fun'

'FRANCIS, F-OFF'

'Robin, how rude of you'

'Francis, please go' said Sandy

'Can't . . . See . . . My feet are stuck to the floor'

Francis made like he tried to lift his foots, but couldn't

'Can't do a thang'

'FRANCIS. I'M WARNIN!'

'Robin, you're so unsociable this evening'

'Said F-OFF, FRANCIS'

'So cold. You're like a stone'

He sipped his drink

'Like a frozen stone'

I shot m'eyes at him

'Well, I am leaving. I can take a hint'

He headed for the door

'You know where I can be found if you feel like having some fun'

He left, then popped his head back in

'And don't do anything BORIS wouldn't do . . . AH HA HA HA'

He headed out. I hopped up, slammed the door, locked it solid and flicked off the light. Sandy and me lay side by side, then I rolled over and planted a soft kiss on Sandy's lips. She lay stairin up. I tried s'more, but the girl stayed stone cold with eyes wide

'Uh Sandy . . . why won't you kiss, huh?'

'Uh-uh'

'But . . . '
'NO'
'But b'fore . . . '
'*Was* before'
'And now . . . '
'Is RIGHT now'
'Awh-h-h Sandy!'
'NO!'

Who wouldn't kiss nohow. After awhile I give up and headed to the kitchen, grabbed some apples and then back into the hall, seein Francis in the control room wavin wildly smilin

The followin mornin we piled into our control seats excited, seein the Moon lookin bigger than before fillin all the front windows and up overhead and off to the sides, with craters everwhere and gold plateaus and hills, dark gulleys and mountain ranges racin into the horizon

Wilbur looked round, with all of us buckled in and said

'Let's get the ole' engines firing'

Then he pressed the glowin orange button on the control counter — but nothin happened. He pressed again. Nothin. He looked round, like all of us. I grinned wide. Wilbur pressed the button — banged it with his fist. He clicked on the mike

'Son of a . . . MISSION CONTROL . . . MISSION CONTROL . . .'

56

He clicked it on, off, on
'MISSION CONTROL . . . . Godamn . . . .FRANCIS
. . . wiring! Boris . . . engines!'
'Aye Aye' said Francis
All hopped up and headed to work

The mornin drifted 'long and there was no progress.
We joined for tea in the kitchen
'What do you think it is?' asked Heather
'Don't know' answered Wilbur 'I only had a bit of engine
training. We're not sure what we're doing'
'I tink linear accelerator vit ionizer' said Bors
'Could be'
'I think we're in a pickle' said Sandy
'Happy-go-be-lucky, Sunday. Remember, alvays happy
-go-be-lucky'
'I've got half the panel apart' said Francis
'How are the computers?' asked Wilbur
'They say MALFUNCTION. But won't tell me where'
'Great!' said Sandy
We sat sippin awhile, watchin the Moon who start-
ed driftin to the side'a the rocket
'Well there she goes, folks . . . the lovely Moon. And
next on our excursion of the Solar System' then Francis
talked real deep 'If you'll unfold your travel brochures'
'Oh No Francis'
Wilbur jumped up, hittin his fist on the table,
startlin everyone

'We'll get us going, and mighty soon. Let's go Boris'
'Yaw'

Bors snickered at Francis

Wilbur swung his head round to the windows like he saw somthn. Then crinkled his brow curious-like

Everyone worked through the day. I offered a hand though the guys said they'd holler, so I went in m'room, got in a cross-leg position and meditated. It's calmin

Sandy and me come down the control stairs after. There was Wilbur covered with grease knittin! I elboed Sandy, then sat in m'seat. Heather was there and Bors smokin a ce-gar

'Knittin, huh?' I asked

'Learned it from my gramma. Been doing it all my life . . . I'm a closet knitter'

Sandy blurted out a small laugh

'There . . . that feels better' Wilbur said

'It's out in the open' added Heather

'You're going to laugh?' he asked

Everyone looked serious. Bors burst out laughin

I was in the hall after when Bors approached covered in grease

'Got her fixed, huh Borsboy?'

'No feex Robeen'

'Gonna get her soon though, huh?'

'No feex'

Bors shook his head. Francis come up

'Vat you vant, flunky flit'

'Oh dunk it, Fido' said Francis

'Nobody talk vit you'

'C'mon Robin, let's have a tea'

'Go sit in flower box vit odder petunias, you fleusy flitball'

'Shut it, filth!'

'Gee Gee Gee Gee' Bors made goofy sounds

'See what an idiot he is?' said Francis

'Gee Gee Gee Gee'

'OK folks, no more of your cornball bickering ... we've got bigger things on our hands' Wilbur 'sclaimed as he come up. Francis swung round and headed to his room, slammed the door. I spotted Sandy in the kitchen bowlin the kettle, and headed in

'Bowlin the kettle, are ya Sandy?'

'Oh Robin, I so hope we get going soon!'

'Oh we will. Sandy, you're the perfect comb'nation of cute 'n sexy'

'That sounds like a line'

'Francis told it to me'

'Am I?'

'Sure. SAY, let's go lay on your bed and stare up at the stars, okay?'

Sandy looked at me. Shook her head. I was grinnin sweet

'Tea, Robin'

So we did

Later the crew stood chattin in the hallway near the kitchen. All'a sudden our jaws dropped. FIVE ALIENS stepped out'a the spacesuits room. Their mouths opened — both crews stood starin at one 'nother
'Boy' I went. I picked up Flower Butt and stepped forward holdin him out — did a false charge. One'a the alien critters pulled out a ballpoint-like thang — pointed — suddenly a beam'a glowin yeller light shot out so's I jumped aside — the light hit a plant vase — it shattered. Me, Francis and Sandy went
'WOAH
WOAH'

Our crew run up the hall, down the stairs to behind the control seats, and ducked low. A big vent screen was beside me. I lifted the screen off, and crawled in
'Hey! C'mon' I said to the others. One by one everyone followed, the skunk and Wilbur last who crawled in backward, then put the screen back
We crawled 'long, hearin the aliens
'Nobody move' said Wilbur
We stayed still — saw a alien head at the top corner'a the vent, he looked in. It was dark in there, so's we could see him — he couldn't see us
The head disappeared. Beside him was a couple aliens laughin wheezy-like, after they bumped the sides'a their butts t'gether

We continued crawlin. I come to n'other vent I pushed in — crawled into the bathroom, follored by the others

We stood packed like possums, Bors in the shower 'Perty convenient' I said 'I mean if ya gotta pee or somthn'

'What do we do?' asked Heather

Wilbur shrugged

'Wait'

After awhile Wilbur 'nounced

'It's been an hour'

'Don't hear nothin' I said

We peeked our heads into the hall

'I t-think they're gone' sputtered Sandy

We creeped up the hall, come to top'a the control steps. The room below was empty

'They're gone Hic' said Sandy. I patted her back

'Where would they go?' asked Heather

'To their ship' answered Wilbur

'Yaw'

'They'll be back' said Francis

'Hope not' I said

So's we sat round the kitchen table, eatin when the galdarn spacesuits room door opens. Six aliens stepped into the hall. Everyone ducked — the aliens walked by and headed down the control stairs

Slowly, carefully, we opened the kitchen door, and duckin low snucked out, me carryin Flower Butt. Sandy tripped — hit me and the skunk, who squealed. The aliens looked up, talked quick, then headed over the stairs

We darted off, into the storage room and slammed the door — locked it

The aliens tried the door handle — chattered on the other side

Then it was quiet s'more

We stood awhile, then sat about
'We gotta think' I said 'They're afraid'a the skunk'
'Wish we had six of them' said Sandy
   Bors opened a box
'Vat's dis?'
   He pulled out big white b'lloons
'Weather balloons' said Wilbur 'for a Moon experiment'
'Yaw'
'Let's . . . Hic' Everyone looked Sandy's way
'Let's . . . I mean . . . I'm an art student'
'Hey!' I went
'If I draw skunks, I mean on these big balloons . . . '
   Bors pulled out felt markers
'Maybe the image will scare them' said Heather
'Right. They might be fraid'a . . . SIX Skunks' I added
'I'd call that a long shot' said Francis
'Could be our only shot' said Wilbur

'Let's try' said Bors

We blowed up the b'lloons and Sandy started drawin with a felt marker — she was t'riffic. A real talent. These big skunks appeared on the white b'lloons

After a bit the engines fired. I went

'Wow, the engines!'

'They fixed them!' 'sclaimed Francis

'Great!' said Sandy while drawin

'Hey, you're real good, Sandy' I said

Later the engines went off

With the six skunk b'lloons we peeked out the door, then creeped up the hall, the b'lloons wavin 'bove us. I carried Flower Butt too for for sure. We approached the top'a the steps over the control room — I cleared m'throat

The aliens, who sat in our seats, perked to attention, then bolted up synchernized — let out wheezy squeals and darted for th'other side'a the room

We headed down the stairs, the big skunk b'lloons waivin above us

The six aliens slid 'long the far wall — kept slidin, and bolted over the stairs, then raced to the spacesuits room and slammed the door

On the monitors we saw the outside door to the ship they left open. Francis used his computer and swung it shut

We all hi-fived, I kissed Flower Butt on the nose

'Flower, ya saved us, ya hairy varmit'

Francis puckered — gave the skunk a big kiss on the nose too

'Long as we have the balloons' said Wilbur, who patted the skunk 'And Flower Butt, I think we're OK'

We all nodded

'Positions' he said. He fired the engines, then turned the ship about, the gold-white Moon come in front'a the windows

After, with the engines off and ship coastin, Sandy 'sclaimed

'Wonder why they're so afraid of the skunk?'

'Maybe they were defeated once by skunk-like creatures' answered Heather

'There are all kinds of critters in space' said Wilbur 'Grasshopper-like, ant-like. So maybe, and why not ﹘ '

'Skunk-like' said Sandy

'Makes sense' said Francis 'Maybe these yellow-green guys have skunk-like creatures for an enemy'

'Whipped their butts once' I added

'Could be' and Heather

After I headed onto m'bed. Heard a knock

'Whoosit?'

'It's Francis. OK if I come in?'

Francis entered, closed the door and flicked on the light. I shot up — bopped m'head off the book shelf

'OUCH!'

'Watch yourself there, tiger'

Francis swung a bottle out from behind his back
'Party time. Got glasses?'
'No. No I don't'
'WEL-L-L, we'll just slug at her like ole' buddies then'
he said gruff-like, nudgin m'shoulder 'Rough it a little'
'Don't drink'
'Sure you do'

He searched in his pants pockets
'Now where did I put that corkscrew?

'It's in your shirt pocket'
'Oh THERE it is. Naughty naughty, hiding on me'

He opened the bottle and took a big slug. His face
lit up — he went 'WHEE!' Offered the bottle
'No thanks'
'Yummy. French wine. Go on' he wiped his mouth
'Uh-uh'

Francis pinched m'butt
'CUT IT OUT, FRANCIS!'
'Oh quiet, quiet. Everyone will hear. They'll want to
crush my nuts with stones'

Francis took a swig, his face lit up
'WAHOOO!'

I hopped up and paced. Francis patted the bed
'C'mon tiger. Sit. Sit. You're making me nervous'

I kep pacin

'Got any glasses?'

'Ain't got none?'

Francis pinched m'butt

'CUT IT OUT!'

'Oh gr-r-r — Ha ha . . . love ya like that'

'Yeah, well QUIT IT'

'Oh-h — so *vicious*' he sipped 'I have it. A MOVIE PARTY. In MY Room. With POPCORN and glasses. Sounds fun Robin? Sit'

I sat

'OK. I'll set everything up. Here, take care of my bottle. No I will'

He headed out the door

'See you in fifteen'

'Oh, sure'

Out as I bolted, combed m'hair real careful, patted on some sweet-smellin stuff and sprayed m'arm pits. I grabbed Flower Butt and headed to Sandy's room. The light was off and place lit by stars. Sandy sat b'side her bed starin out the window

'Some stars, hu Sandy?'

'They're beautiful. I'm so releived, I mean, we have the engines back. The yellow guys have left'

'Yeah, great. SAY — let's lay on your bed and stare up at the stars, OK?'

'Wel-l-l'

Sandy and me lay side by side. I hopped up — locked the door solid. We started kissin hot, comin hotter.

We started squirmin, rippin each other's clothes off. I mounted Sandy and did m'duty as a male to the species. And I was good. Boy was I good. Sandy was screamin and I was thrustin. Hope the others didn't hear. Who cares. It was three points for the guy side

I was hopin after she didn't get pregnant, 'cause I wasn't wearin no glove. It is the female's part to take care of that angle, ain't it?

We lay back after listenin to soft music Sandy played. A knock come on the door

Knock   Knock Knock 'You in there Robin?'

'Shh Sandy, Shh'

'I can hear you. Said you'd come to my room' 'sclaimed Francis

'No I didn't'

'Open the door, it's locked'

'Tee hee' Sandy giggled

'Ha ha ha' I laughed

'Open this bloody door!'

Francis shook the knob

'Ah ha ha, lego Sandy'

'Ha ha'

'What are you two doing? Robin, OPEN THIS FREAK-ING DOOR'

'Oh yeah, Francis, thanks though'

'What do you mean *thanks though*. Look, everything's set up in my room for our movie party'

'Tee hee'

'Ah ha ha'

'Will you two STOP!'

'Tee hee'

'Ah ha ha ha'

  He kicked the door

'Oh-h! Tell you what. I'll get another glass. Prepare *more* popcorn. And a space for you too, Sandy. So get ready, OK?'

'Ha ha, lego Sandy'

'Ah ha'

'ROBIN, DID YOU HEAR ME?'

'AH HA HA . . . OOEE SANDY, HO HO'

'Oh, this is so stupid!'

  He kicked the door again

'Did you hear me Robin!?'

'Oh shore Francis, thanks'

'OK, we'll see you in ten minutes'

'Ho ho Sandy, stopt'

'Tee hee'

  Francis left as Sandy and me tore to one another s'more, makin wild FURIOUS love. We lay back after, and Francis knocked

 Bomp   Bomp Bomp 'You in there, Robin?' Bomp

  He shook the knob

'Shh Sandy, shh'

'Don't shush. I've everything prepared . . . Robin!'

'Oh hi Frantificus'

'Fran-who?'

'It's Roman'

Sandy laughed, tickled me

'Ha ha Sandy, lego ha ha'

'Ho ho'

'Will you two CUT THAT OUT!'

'AH HA HA HA'

'HEE HEE HEE HEE'

'OPEN THIS FUCKING DOOR!'

'OOEE SANDY, HO HO'

'TEE HEE'

'OH HO HO! DIP DA DIP DIP DIP'

Francis kicked the door, who left. Sandy and me made HOT VICIOUS love s'more, and on the evernin wore

Followin mornin we all joined in the control room, Sandy and me tickled toes on top'a the counter, giggled, tossed nuts to Flower Butt. Skunk b'lloons floated 'bove us. Wilbur was loaded with grease, bags b'low his eyes all bloodshot, lookin like he hadn't slept. Heather and Francis smoked continuous

After we headed in the kitchen carryin the b'lloons — had coffee, toast and cereal. Bors poured into his cup from a small bottle in a paper bag. Flower Butt tried to climb up Sandy's leg who she lifted to her lap and petted
'I think he likes me' she said. I smiled
　　Francis ate advocadoes
'Avocado comes from a Native word meaning testicle'

'Don't say' said Heather

'Do . . . Fact'

'Francis, pass the salt'

   He passed it to Sandy, and continued

'Speaking about *testicles*, which hangs lower, the left ball or the right? . . . Hum?'

'Who cares' said Bors

'I do. It's important'

'Right' said Sandy

'Wrong'

'The left' I said

'Right'

'Huh?' went Wilbur

   I looked in m'Fantastic Facts book

'Says some people has tape worms 30 foot long that live in their guts'

'How long?' asked Wilbur

'30 foot. Some has 15, 10 footers'

'How can that be? How long are our intestines?' asked Sandy

'The size of a tennis court' said Heather

'WHAT' me 'n Sandy went

'If you stretch them all out, about that long'

'VOW!'

'They eats your food' I said

'Boris probably has a 50 footer' said Francis

'Yeah . . . !'

'I saw another worm fact in the book. It's a lovely. Pass it please, Robin'

I passed the book — Francis flipped through

'Oh here it is!'

'Hold on!' said Sandy

'There's another worm, a round worm, which lives in intestines, humans, and can . . . get this . . . if it wants . . . Here it comes . . . '

'Yaw?'

'The worm can crawl out of your nose if it feels the urge. So say you're having dinner with the queen . . . '

'Vat . . . dvrag queen?'

'Yes, very formal, and this worm comes dangling out of your nose? And just hangs there, checking things out. Truthfully, I don't think they'd invite you back'

'Me neither' said Sandy

'This for real?' asked Wilbur

Francis showed the book

'LOOK. See . . . worm . . . out nose'

He looked back in the book

'There's more. Sometimes they tickle your throat. If you cough up, they can blast into your mouth! Some are *a foot long!*'

Francis closed the book. Looked round. We just sat stairin

'Eat. Eat your food!' he said

'My GAWD!' went Wilbur

'So if you feel a tickling in your throat, there's a good chance worms are wiggling around there. Ever feel a tickling in your throat?'

'No!' went Heather

'No' said Sandy, shakin her head

'Nope' I said

'NO!' said Wilbur

'All time' went Bors

'YES YOU HAVE! So don't blame me if a worm comes wiggling out of your mouth. You were warned'

'End of topic' said Heather

'Eat your food'

'Thanks Francis' Sandy said

'*Better informed than sorry*'

    We just sat

'HEATHER! What's that in your nose?' asked Sandy

'My pet miniature frog. That's where he lives'

'What's his name?' I asked

'Maynard'

    We looked at each other. I blowed a big gum bubble and popped it

'Robin, don't do that' Sandy said. Francis headed to the fridg'rater — pulled out a box'a pastries, took a big scoop'a whip cream off a pastry, licked his finger

'Care for a peach pecan, Robie?' he asked

'No thanks'

'Apple square, pear delight?'

'Uh-uh, thanks though'

'How about a -- '

'Shallup, fleusy'

'Ignore. So Robin, would you like a chocolate chunky with nuts?'

'Yaw, like you . . . Nut'

Francis looked to the ceilin, spread his hands

'Love thy brother' then continued 'Robin, how about a cherry square?'

'Vy you no sit in flower box vit odder petunias, fee fee flit'

Francis glared at Bors. Sandy started to hiccup

'They ask vat I vont on trip, I say fvruit and nuts, and they give you, all in vun package'

Sandy kept hiccupin

'Think you're superior, just because I had a late puberty. Is that it?' asked Francis

'Bah'

'Somebody told you?'

'Fleusy'

'UP YOURS, CUNT! AND DON'T LEAVE HAIRS IN THE BATHROOM SINK! So Robin, how about -- WHAT'S THAT OUT THERE?!'

He pointed. We all swung round — jaws dropped

A long, copper-brown craft with yeller lights round floated to the side'a our ship

'What the hell!' 'sclaimed Wilbur

'WHAT IS IT?' blurted Heather

'A . . . space . . . craft' went Sandy

'One of ours?' I asked

Wilbur shook his head

'Doesn't look like it'

'Holy . . . . tomatoes!' 'sclaimed Francis

'Yaw'

The craft just floated 'long to the rear of our ship

Suddenly the pastry box rised out'a Francis' hands, follered by Francis and all of us up off our seats, 'long with the cups and dish water. We floated round in the air

'Gravity's gone' said Wilbur, who shrugged funny, then kicked his way out the door and up the hall to the engine room. We started gettin wet, figured it was dryer in the control room. We dog-paddled and float-ed clumsy out the door and into the control area. Papers floated about. Bors grabbed the big rubber plant in center'a the room — stayed with both foots aimed to the ceilin, dandruffs sprayin round his head

Sandy reached over as we floated about — tried to tickle me

'Cut it out, Sandy! Ha ha'

Wilbur said he fiddled with some wires in the engine room, then fell to the floor. He heard thumps other side'a the engines

Headed over, sneaked round the engines but found nothin

In the control room we all crashed to the floor
Returnin, Wilbur asked
'Everyone OK?'
'No, no broke bones' said Bors
'Such rotten luck!' went Francis
'Bah, cupcake'

We was in our rooms. I headed off and knocked on
Sandy's door. She sat in her position on the floor
against the bed, stairin at stars
'Y'know Sandy, ever tell ya I'd like to be a movie star?'
'So would I'
'Really?'
'U-huh'
'Yeah, like, I wanna sail round the world, see lots'a
stuff . . . and save the planet and all — but wow, bein
a movie idol!'
'U-huh'
'Got the looks, right?'
'You're a creep'
    I tickled Sandy, who swerved aside
'So what's your philosophy, Robin?'
'Be lovin. To animals . . . plants . . . and people'
    She nodded, said
'Mine is live from the heart. Do what you love'
'That's beautiful. Say Sandy, speakin 'bout — SAY, let's
lay on the bed and stare up at the stars, OK?'
Well . . . '

I pulled her over, and planted a kiss on Sandy's lips, then another. Sandy wouldn't kiss

'It's the situation, huh? Reason you won't kiss?'

'Wel-l-l . . . '

'Cause you're nervous, right?'

'Yes and, umm . . . '

'Um what, huh Sandy?'

'Well . . . '

'Well what, huh Sandy?'

'Well, I was thinking'

'Ya, thinkin's good'

'And, well, it's something I never told you before, Robin'

'Oh?'

    She nodded

'U-huh. Back home . . . promise you won't become sore'

'Sore! Me become sore. Hah! So what's the big secret, huh Sandykins?'

'Well-l, I have a boyfriend Robin. We've been seeing each other a whole *six months* now'

    I popped up, m'eyes bulged

'Oh Robin, you aren't sore?'

'Hah! ME, SORE? . . . So you have a BOYFRIEND!'

'Yes and ‒‒ '

    I cut in — m'eye twitched big time

'So Sandy has a *boyfriend*'

'Oh Robin'

'Whose sore!'

'You are. You're neck is red, and your ears . . . '

   I stood

'So, little bit'a news . . . Sandy has a FREAKIN *boyfriend!*'

   I heads to the door

'Robin, don't go'

'Why not? I'll leave ya alone ta play with yourself while ya look at your boyfriend's piture'

'ROBIN!'

'So long Ms Sidewalk'

   I slammed the door

Next mornin in bed I looked at the clock — it spinned backwards. I got up and banged the thang but no use. Then I stumbled over a sneaker and crashed to the wall. All the ship's lights went out

Poked m'head out the door. Nobody. I headed up the hall. It was lit with a few dim emergency lights. All a sudden I shot m'eyes to the ceilin. 'Cause Sandy climbed over the stairs comin up the hall from the other direction. I whistled, whipped m'head to the right wall like I saw somthn real interestin — she passed by on left

Headed into the bathroom, then control room. The lights come on. Bors was in the kitchen with a plastic bag filled with ice cubes tied to his head. Could see him through the glass pourin popcorn on a slice'a

bread, then a slice'a cheese, tomater and lettuce, he poured on katsup and may'naise. A squirt'a may'naise hit the floor. He carried the samwich to his seat, slipped on the may'naise and everythin went flyin. He let out a loud
'Fock!'

Francis come in the kitchen who started slicin at the sideboard. He and Bors yelled who we could hear in the control room. Francis froze all of a sudden, throwed the tomater he was holdin at Bors who ducked b'low the table. The tomater splattered red and slid down the glass wall

Francis throwed the knife onto the chops block. It bounced up and stuck in the bottom'a the cupboard above where it waddled back and forth. He whipped round, flung Bors the finger and stormed out the door
'FUCKER!'

Bors popped up, whirled his thumb round in his coffee cup — continued eatin

Back in the control room, Heather sat b'side Wilbur who was knittin. Bors come down the stairs and looked at him
'It calms my nerves' sclaimed Wilbur
'Vat nerves?'

Bors swigged from a small bottle in a paper sack. Francis come down the stairs
'We just want some love' I said 'We all want love . . .

more than anythin else'

Heather nodded. I looked to Francis

'He wants love, Francis, give him some love'

'You vant me throw up' sclaimed Bors

'Love him, Francis' said Heather. Francis made a sour face

'Love me' said Bors. Francis got up and left. I shrugged

After we was all in the kitchen. Skunk b'lloons floated over the seats

'Finding these balloons was so serendipity' said Francis

'Huh?' I asked

'It was very serendipity'

'Sera-what?' asked Sandy

'Dipity'

'Like you. Dipstick' said Bors

'OK FOLKS' went Wilbur

'Francis, what does serendipity mean?' asked Heather

'Serendipity, *stupids*, is when you have luck with something, as in finding it accidentally'

'Yup, them b'lloons was seredpitus'

'Dipity'

'Here we go again' said Sandy

We wasn't talkin. I forgot and asked

'Say Sandy, have you seen my . . . . Oh, Wilbur, could you ask Sandy if she's got my Mighty White Clipboard?'

'OK Robin . . . Sandy' Wilbur cleared his throat 'Do

you have Robin's Mighty White Clipboard?'

He smiled round

'I do Wilbur, and will return it when I can'

'Oh yeah?'

'Yeah . . . and Wilbur, could you ask *Robin* if he has my Heavenly Sounds CD?'

'Do Wilbur, and will return it pronto, 'cause I've no use for it nohow!'

'OH YEAH!'

'YEAH!'

'Well Wilbur, *you can tell* Robin . . . . oh-h, never mind!'

'Oh Yeah! Never mind too!'

Both of us sat side by side fumin, all the others chuckled into their hands, glanced 'bout. I blowed a big gum bubble, then popped it loud. Did another, popped it. Blowed 'nother s'more. Wilbur aimed a small knife t'ward it, so I swung round to Sandy and popped it at her. She got up and went to the sideboard

I started chawin the gum real loud lookin at her, she let out a small snicker and headed to the door. Hah!

After supper I lay on my bed — heard a knock

Kn_ock   Kn_ock

'WHOOSIT?'

'It's Sandy'

'So!'

'So can I come in?'

'Choose your pick'

Sandy entered wearin m'fav'rite yeller shirt, her hair combed up fancy. She smiled sweet

'I have your clipboard'

'OH, IT'S YOU!'

I hopped up — bashed m'head off the book shelf

'OUCH!'

'Watch yourself there, Robin'

'Can place it on the dresser. I'll return your CD at m'leisure'

'I want to talk'

'Yeah? 'Bout what!'

I eased on a elbow

'Wel-l-l . . . it's about –– '

'Yeah . . . and you was talkin yesterday'

'Oh-h! It's about my *boyfriend*'

I bolted up, eyes bulged

'So how's your boyfriend, huh Sandy!'

'Calm down Robin. I was thinking . . . and . . . I like you a lot, you know'

'So'

'Oh-h, like, well . . . . he isn't my boyfriend any longer'

'OH?'

She shook her head

'And I do like you a lot'

'Sandy, there's somthn I have to confess'

'There *is*?'

I nodded

'There's 'nother lady in m'life, you know. Who I sat b'side ofin in the park'

'You HAVE?'

'And she has beautiful limbs, and curves'

'She DOES?'

'And Sadie's one'a the most beautiful ladies I know'

'SAD — you mean . . . THE OAK TREE?'

    I laughed. Sandy pushed me. I took her in m'arms, flinged her head back swash-bucklin like, and planted a whopper kiss on Sandy's sugar lips

Followin mornin Heather roused us all into the control room for calisthentics, to get in shape for landin on the Moon next day. Everyone touched noses, wiggled toes, raced up the stairs barefoots, round the kitchen table up the hall and round the rubber plant in the control room, back over the stairs and long the hall — Bors and Flower Butt trailed behind. After we lay pleadin and pantin on the control room carpet, 'cause Heather turned into one VICIOUS phys'cal 'structor

Later Sandy and me rose up the tel'scope on the counter — Sandy scoped and I jotted notes. Both of us looked at the clock as it hit one bein the signal. I bolted up, and peered round suspicious-like, tugged m'earlobe to Sandy who nodded. I mouthed some 'structions and dashed over the stairs, up the hall and into the mop closet. Sandy follered after a bit. We poked our heads out the closet door seein all was clear, and slid 'long the wall, into the bathroom and had a shower t'gether

Bors perpared supper that day — all of us hopped on our seats swishin hands havin rip-roarin appetites. But we sat twirlin our forks slower and slower, pushin rock-hard peas round cold mash taters filled with lumps. Tried to cut into the lambs chops which was hard like rubber, scooped into borsht beet soup which was loaded with peppers, lungin for water glasses and gulpin. Bors bopped the bottom'a the pepper shaker and slurped bowl after plate. He asked why we wasn't eatin — we said caus'a bein so excited over landin on the Moon. After we cleared the plates for pie, with all of us divin in — then stopped. Bors' rhubarbs pie tasted saar like burnt rubber boots. Everyone pushed our plates away, smiled, chawed cel'ry sticks. Bors twinkled his eyes, who we complimented on the color-filled supper

Later me and Flower Butt joined Sandy in her room where we sat on the floor, our backs 'gainst the bed. Sandy petted Flower Butt in her lap
'I'm so excited' she said 'I don't know if I'll be able to

sleep tonight'

'Yeah, landin should be fun'

'The Moon's so beautiful'

'Yeah. Say, ever tell ya of the time I couldn't sleep for three days, and nights too I was so excited'

'Nope'

'Yup, it happened last summer, on a sunny mornin. I was strollin up a country road, thinkin deep, sayin to m'self, boy, y'know, it's all the same, I mean, all colors, flavors, animals, everythin has this same distinc' ingredient in it, ya know, all has this special somthn, like, it's all one, ya know'

Sandy nodded

'I was sayin this, thinkin deep, when all of a sudden m'head went POP, just like that, and it was like there wasn't a head on m'shoulders, like I could feel breezes up there'

'Wow'

'And I stood lookin about, and everythin was shimmerin Sandy, I mean the stones, the trees, everythin I could see was alive, and conscious, like it was lookin at me'

'Oh WOW'

'And I stood watchin, with m'mouth open, like seein for the first time, feelin like a little kid standin there'

'Oh boy'

'And everythin was sparklin, Sandy, and so alive, and I felt so joyous, and started writin poems after that,

I mean poems just come rumblin up'

'WOW Robin'

'And I stayed natural stoned for three months, and then come real low, and, well, come out'a it . . . and . . . here I am'

'Boy Robin. I wish I could experience something like that'

'Yeah'

So I headed to my room after to get lots'a rest for landin on the Moon tomorrow

Followin mornin we awoke excited, hopped into our control seats watchin the golden Moon glowin close-up in front'a the ship. Wilbur whipped on the engines to slow us — we went saurin into the Moon's grav'ty grip. Coasted over craters and canyons and rock mountain ranges stairin through b'noc'lars. Then on to the night side with stars shinin all around, the dark brown scenery comin carmel and then gold, the Sun popped over the horizon as we coasted to the day-side again, cross craters. We looked at moon maps 'There it is! Our landin spot' I 'sclaimed

Wilbur fired the engines, gripped the steerer as we aimed t'ward this wide crater. Said
'Ship's supposed to land upright and on her butt if we do this correct'

We zeroed in to center of the crater — lowered — the bottom'a the ship hit the crater floor — we bounced ^{up} down ^{up} down

Dust swirled round the windows. We looked at each other, shook up

'Whew!' I went

'My first landing' said Wilbur

'Went lovely' said Francis as he eased his collar

'Let's get this baby upright' continued Wilbur

Three legs spread out side'a the ship, and started pushin the ole' baby up erect 'till Spaceship Faithful sat on her butt

We hi-fived — raced over the stairs to the spacesuits room and climbed into our white outfits. Lowered big clear bubble helmits, havin a gold coatin, snapped them solid, attached colored hoses to our chest from backpacks. We all waddled into the compression room and sat on benches watchin the suits puff round us

Pressed the button b'side the oval door, heard

'First floor, ladies' lingerie, sleepware, bedding'

Wilbur banged the button and the door slowly swung open. We popped our helmits out, gasped at the gorgeous Moon scenery. It was quiet, and still, and 'lectric surrounded by stars, like bein inside a giant light bulb. We realized our stairs hadn't come out as s'posed to, so we pressed the button, then closed the door and opened it s'more — heard

'Second floor -- '

Wilbur walloped the button — still no stairs

'Damn stairs won't come out'

'What do we do?' asked Sandy

All a sudden Bors' face lit up

'OOH! OOH!'

'I think Boris just had a great idea' said Heather

'Or his Ex Lax finally kicked in' said Francis

'Ve build vrope ladder'

'Terrific idea, Boris' 'sclaimed Wilbur

Bors grinned wide. We waddled up the hall, into the storage room, collected rope we spread over the hall carpet, and cut and tied a long orange ladder which we carried to the compression room. Tied one end to the benches and dropped her out the door — hit ground perfec. We hi-fived and climbed out the ship, into the sunshine and starshine and blue and white planet shine who's right half was glowin above us. Down the rope ladder, all facin the rocket holdin a skunk b'lloon on a stick. We stepped our foots to the ground, looked round 'stonished — it all glowed gold-en-like, and peaceful-feelin like almost it was watchin us, the boulders and crater rocks and this rock mountain range which raced into the horizon

We hopped about, gettin the feel in our white puffed-out suits, hoppin higher and higher, feelin so ex'hilerous. After we gathered, checked each other's fly packs was on right, pressed buttons on our chests

— dust shot out at our foots — all of us rised up off the ground beside the rocket and saured higher and higher. We flicked levers and shot forward with arms spread, b'lloons floatin behind us, we went skimmin over the crater, up o'er its rim and clipped 'long, 'cross the glitterin Moon scenery, swirled down into a deep dark gulley we 'splored about, up over it's edge into the sunshine s'more, cross a flat plateau, over some hills. After we headed back toward the towerin white rocket ship, whirled round and round, then touched our foots soft on the ground

We giggled to each other 'cited in our bubbles, then climbed the ladder and snored on the benches and floors

We raced into the kitchen havin snacks. I flipped a pickle up round m'back and caught it in m'mouth

Then with a skunk b'lloon attached to a stick we gathered in the compression room, puffed the suits and pressed open the door — pushed the button to eject our moon buggy . . . the gawd dang thang didn't come out like s'posed. Wilbur banged the button though nothin as the voice said

'Sixth floor, men's bathroom –– '

Bors hurled his shoulder at the panel

'Co-operate, bitch you!'

'Cool her, Borisboy' said Francis

'Maybe we can find another way' s'ggested Wilbur

96

'Let's carry it over the rope ladder' said Heather

'Will it fit through the door?' asked Sandy

'Let's give it a try' said Wilbur

All of us nodded, waddled to the buggy chamber. We was able to lift her out and carried the baby to the compression room, tied ropes to her. Wilbur and Francis headed out first holdin on from bottom as we eased the buggy out the door. Sandy, me, Heather and Bors lowered her with ropes from on top, we got the baby to the ground perfec!

We climbed down with our stick b'lloons

The brown-yeller UFO craft hovered over some mountains

We climbed aboard the buggy but the front rised into the sky, realizin it was too heavy in the back with everybody, so I s'ggested

'Hey, how 'bout you guys have her this evenin — can have a romantic cruise'

I winked to Heather and Wilbur. Wilbur looked at Heather and chuckled

Francis and Bors climbed in the back, Sandy the front b'side me in the driver's seat. I pressed the button and dust shot out as the buggy rised. I pulled a lever and we saured forward, wavin back to Heather and Wilbur. We skimmed over rocks and boulders, up over the crater wall and 'long a flat plateau, up over 'nother crater we continued swishin 'cross the golden scenery like on a magic carpet

'Oh this is such glorious countryside' Click Click Click

Francis took pitures

'Wait till the gang sees these back home'

'Vat gang?'

Sandy looked at the moon map on her lap, and pointed

'Let me see, that must be Cracker Creek, um-um, has to be Baldee's Bluff over there, no Billy's . . . '

'Ve no lost, hey naveegator?'

'Oh no Bors, Sandy's the best nav'gator this side'a . . . Uranus. Ain'tcha?'

'No, it has to be . . . '

'Know vhere vee go, yaw naveegator?'

''Course she does'

But Sandy turned into one lousy moon mapper, and we was lost, stopped in center of a wide crater

After awhile Francis reached out his hand and said 'Tag!', who hopped off the buggy and I hopped after and chased him. With his hands hangin in front, Francis tippy-toed and run goofy-like. Sandy and Bors joined in too as the four'a us chased one 'nother round boulders, cross the crater playin touch. We felt light there on the Moon, like kids havin fun

After awhile the spaceship cruised over the crater wall, and landed clumsy in center. We all ducked b'low a big boulder — heard a voice in our bubbles

'OK, we know you're hiding there behind that big boulder'

'Ha Ha'

'Shh . . . Sandy . . . Shh . . . he knows where we are'

'Oh yes, everyone out. It's suppertime, and Sandy's turn again to be . . . COOK FOR A DAY'

'Oh yeah!'

Sandy popped up

'Garsh!' I said

'Vee have such fun!'

'Oh yes, but you can play later' said Wilbur

Francis reached out his hand, touchin Bors

'Tag'

He raced away and Bors chased him

After we chased each other over the ladder, and lay snorin on the compression room benches and floors

When supper was over we carried lawn chairs down the rope ladder, spread them in a sem-eye circle, and sat stairin up at the big beautiful blue and white plan-et, the skunk b'lloons 'bove us. White wispy clouds floated oer em'rald oceans and continents on the right half lit up from the bright Sun, with white polar caps appearin so awesome. A line'a laundry hung from the ship to a pole in the ground b'hind us

'Fifty percent of 'Mericans don't know how long it takes Earth to go round the Sun' I said

'So how long?' asked Heather

'Three days' said Sandy

'Five. I know. I scientist' said Bors

'So it's five' Heather smiled round. Glancin up I said
'Glor'yous, ain't momma Earth?'
'Sure is, hillbilly'
    I looked at Francis
'Y'know, with this accent I just open m'mouth, and
people start deductin IQ points'
'Hum . . . ' went Wilbur
'Figures they can pick m'pockets when I ain't lookin.
HAH! I'm as intelligent as . . . Eisenstein'
'It's Einstein' said Sandy, who elbowed me
'Ooph!'
'No you ain't'
'Einstein Boris, one of your confreres, a fellow scien-
tist' said Francis
'Von of my cornflakes? I don't eat dose'
'I give up'
'Yaw, should. Shoot yourself'
'Albert Einstein never wore socks' said Wilbur
'Isn't that unsanitary?' asked Heather 'You get ath-
lete's feet, or foot'
'Foots' I corrected her
'Thank you Robin'
'So I guess Einstein had smelly athlete's foots' Francis
said, noddin to me 'See, he wasn't perfect'
'Could have done with a haircut too' added Wilbur
'Bad hair and smelly feet. I'd never date him' contin-
ued Francis. Heather said
'He had a crush on Marilyn Monroe'

'Really?' went Wilbur

'Read it'

'Lovesick. And bad hair and smelly, rotting feet. And this was *thee* Einstein' 'sclaimed Francis

'It's Eisenstein' I corrected him

'Thank you, mister foots'

'He said the universe was friendly' 'sclaimed Heather

'At times I wonder' pondered Sandy

'I think it's friendly' I said

'I guess'

Lookin up at the big blue planet, Wilbur asked

'Y'ever stop to think how many people are doing it right now?'

'Doing what?' asked Sandy

'Washing their laundry' said Heather

'Vy you vant know that?'

Wilbur smiled to Heather

'Just curious'

'Lots. Vit machine. By hand'

We all chuckled. Francis asked

'Do you do yours by hand?'

'All time' said Bors

'I like doing mine in a group' said Francis

'In laudreymat?'

'That's right. In the rear'

'Vy rear? Vy not machine?'

'It's more fun'

Sandy looked up at the planet

'Francis, if you could have anything in the world, what would you choose?'

'To meet another guy who looks just like me'

'We're not conceited, are we?' asked Heather

'Of course not' said Sandy

'It would be heaven'

'Boris, what would you choose?' asked Heather

'I be king, have slaves all around'

'Oh?' went Wilbur

'Yaw, dey fan me all day, clip my toenails'

'Nose hairs' added Francis

'Yaw, give massage all time ven I snap fingers, bathe, cook feed me'

'Sounds like a plan . . . creep slob'

'Vat you be, pvrincess?'

'OK now. Wilbur, what would you do?' asked Heather

'Think I'd live on my own tropical island, surrounded by luscious island babes'

'Oh?'

'I'd save the planet' I said

'A nobler one' went Heather

'Sure, feed everyone, clean up the mess'

'Sandy, you'd . . . ?' asked Heather

'I'd be similar to Robin. I'd sprinkle cleaning dust, healing rays from clouds which I'd float around on'

'Onto Wilbur's island with his tropical women slaves?' asked Heather

'No, they're just honey babes' said Wilbur

After chattin we gathered round the buggy and watched Wilbur rise up seated b'side Heather — both floated off — all of us waved. Bors and Francis yawned, and climbed up the rope ladder. Sandy and me strolled hand in hand, perched on a big boulder where we stared to the huge blue and white planet which looked so romantic. I felt HOT things for Sandy, and said some too

'Glor'yous, ain't it Sugar Baby?'

'It's awesome'

'Sandy, I'd walk a tightrope for you'

'You'd . . . '

'Sure, Buttercup'

'Oh'

'Sandy, you're m'tulip from heaven'

'I . . . am?'

'M'heart's on fire'

'OH ROBIN, YOU'RE SO-O ROMANTIC'

Then we walked hand in hand to the rope ladder, climbed over and to Sandy's room, where we made *smooth* hot love on top'a the Moon

I popped m'head out the door after, heard snorin from Bors' room, sneaked up the hall bare-ass neked to the kitchen. Grabbed some apples and glasses'a water, and strolled out the door when ALL OF A SUDDEN LAUGHTER AND GIGGLES COME OUT THE SPACESUITS ROOM, then Heather and Wilbur stepped into the hall

I continued t'ward them

'Oh hi' I said real casual 'Have a nice float?'

'It was —— ' started Heather

'Awesome' said Wilbur

'Yeah, fun huh?'

'Is it ever!' said Heather

'Robin, where are your —— ?'

Started Wilbur. Heather elbowed him

'Ooph . . . '

'Out for a stroll, to the storage room . . . THAT'S IT . . . do some inventory' I said

'I see . . . ' said Wilbur

I bit in the apple, sipped water the same time — m'face red like lobsters. I passed by, and stepped a foot into the storage room. Wilbur went

'HEY ROBIN'

'Yeah?'

'COOL, DUDE!'

He give me a thumbs up

'Oh, u-huh'

I smiled, bit the apple and stepped in

Next mornin we awoke 'cited. Sittin in the kitchen I watched Wilbur and Heather come out'a her room in bath robes. Later the crew gathered in the control room, then bounced one another off the hall wall, racin to the spacesuits room. Over the ladder we went carryin 'speriments we set on the Moon floor 'long with the skunk b'lloons. Sandy and I uncapped the tel'scope and did a pile'a scopin, bein great on the Moon cause the atmosphere up there is clear. Bors was off to the side'a the ship surrounded with 'speriments

After we gathered round the rocket, checked each other's fly packs, pressed buttons and rised up off the ground, flicked levers we saured forward o'er the gold Moon scenery, six white seagulls floatin 'long with arms spread

In a hour we sailed back and swirled and whirled round the ship, touched our foots to the ground and hi-fived

We gathered the 'speriment stuff and headed up the ladder WHEN ALL OF A SUDDEN THE COPPER-BROWN SHIP ZEROED T'WARD US. We watched with mouths open droppin thins, raced up the ladder into the spaceship one by one and slammed the door. Headed into the control room and stood lookin at the alien craft
'Let's get the hell out'a here' said Wilbur
'Good suggestion' s'ggested Heather
    He pressed the orange button — nothin happened! He tried again — nothin
    Our jaws dropped. Wilbur slammed his fist on the panel — a ROAR thundered out'a the engines, and dust rised round us
'Hah, that's better!'
    Wilbur kissed the button, then pulled on the lever as the ship rised up ᵘᵖ off the Moon floor, speeded faster, away from the Moon's grav'ty grip, we aimed at the glowin blue and white planet in front, and Sun off to the right side which lit her up, and us inside our ship. Looked like the copper-brown craft was long gone

'So Boris, make any notable scientific discoveries while on the Moon?' asked Wilbur as we sat in the kitchen after supper sippin tea

'Oh yaw'

'Can you say?' asked Heather

'Certain, I find as all previous teories, dee Moon . . . is definately made . . . of cheese'

'Oh?' asked Wilbur

'Sviss cheese'

'I see our mission has been quite a success then, scientifically speaking' 'sclaimed Wilbur

'Oh yaw'

   All of us laughed

'Some guys have two penises, did you know?' commented Francis

'Nope' said Sandy

'Yeah. Can be side by side, or on top of each other'

'Hum . . . ' I went. Looked in m'Fantastic Facts book

'Says here. Remember — how many people are doin it? Wilbur's question on the Moon?'

'Laundry' said Bors

'Right. Says at any moment, given the count of people on the planet, and computer calc'lations, four THOUSAND people, or two THOUSAND couples, are doin it at any moment'

'Laundry' went Bors again

'Right' said Francis, who took the book

'Wow' went Wilbur

'Which grows faster, fingernails or toenails?' asked Francis

'Both the same' I said

'Wrong'

'Toenails?' asked Sandy. Francis throwed out his thumb and index finger in a circle

'Wrong. Answer — Fingernails grow four times faster than toenails'

'So' I said

'So there'

Bors headed to the refrig'rater, poked his head in and poked round. Francis flipped through the book

'Here it is. Get this! A GORILLA'S erect *dork* is . . . clue — a bull's is three fabulous feet long, so a gorilla's is . . . guess — two feet, one and one half . . . twelve inches?'

'Twelve inches' said Sandy

'WRONG. A gorilla's erect love muscle is only, ready? TWO INCHES in all its most powerful, glorious manliness'

'Perty small' I said

'About the size of Boris" said Francis

Bors come to attention at the 'frig'rator

'Vat?'

'Talking about your pride and joy' said Francis

'My degree from university?'

'That's it. It's two inches long'

'No, bigger'

'Don't lie'

'Vy lie, is lot bigger'

    Heather laughed. I said

'Gorillas can weigh up to 500 pounds'

'That's a lot' said Heather

'And his dickie's only two inches — hard!'

'That's HARD to believe' said Wilbur

'I don't find it so hard' answered Francis

'I find it hard' said Sandy

'This is HARDLY a topic for space-travelling intellectuals' and Heather

'Who hintillectual? Hard to believe Francees hintellectual'

'Chew me'

'See . . . hard'

'And so our HARD conversation dries up and withers 'way' I said

'It's HARDly a whimper' added Sandy

'Hard to part with it' and Heather

'I can't stand it any longer!' Wilbur pulled his hair

'HARDEN up tough guy' I said 'You're an astroNUT'

    Again we saw the alien ship through the window. I asked

'Whata they want?'

'Ah!' Bors waved his hand 'No vory'

'Um Francis, could I have some tea?' Sandy handed

the pot to Francis 'It's empty'

Francis peeked an eyeball in

'**TEA**. TEA she says. Why for such a lovely as thee, I'd swim the deepest oceans, crawl the burning desserts. **TEA**. TEA she asks, why I'd fight ferocious dragons, scale the highest mountains, I'd . . . swim . . . '

'Said that one' said Heather

'TEA! she says'

'It appears you have a rival, Robin' said Heather

'Of this I'm well aware. And been polishin m'duelin pistols'

'EEK! Another skirmish!'

'You speak correct, Oh famed Francis of the trail'a broken hearts'

'YIKES, Oh save me Sir Boris'

'Vat, me?'

'Pray, save me, fair princess'

'Scale mountain cliffs, huh bub?' went Sandy

'YIKES, oh mercy, kind sir, cute defender of the good'

'Well, well ifin yee be quick. For my sweet has thirst, does thee not sweet'

'Oh yay, yay' went Sandy

'So beoff, 'less I swipe off a toe'

'Oh thank you, kind sir, gallant defender of the good'

Francis bended forward and kissed m'hand.

Everone applauded

'Vat's vit kissing?'

'It's apropos' said Francis

'Apre-what?' asked Heather
'Apre popo' I said
'Apricots' said Sandy
'Apropos, stupids' 'sclaimed Francis
'Talk Henglish' said Bors
'As if you'd understand'
'Jerk'
'Meathead'
'OK folks' cut in Wilbur

After we gathered in Sandy's room who was chosen hostess — Sandy carried hot apples cider for us to sip. We was chattin on the carpet, and singin, then raised arms up round the shoulders'a the ones beside us, smiled happy sailin through the stars

I swatted a fly, dreamin it was crawlin up m'arm, over m'shoulder. Then I twitched m'nose, tryin to sleep. Sandy kept strokin a white feather 'cross m'face and down m'body. I heard her giggle and popped an eye open — lept up — throwed her over on the bed, and that mornin we started the day off with a bang!

After we poked our heads out the door, heard snorin from Bors' room figurin it was real early
'Everybody's sleeping' said Sandy
'Bet we can make the shower and back bare butt'
Me an Sandy hi-fived and creeped up the hall tip-toein 'long, shushin to one other with our index fingers gigglin 'way. We come to where the wall on left broke to glass, with the kitchen behind, where Heather,

Wilbur and Francis sat at the table with s'prised looks on their faces. Sandy and me glanced at each other, dropped to the palms of our foots and walked normal, tossed waves to the gang, and headed right into the bathroom

We bent forward and laughed, then after havin a shower poked our heads through the door seein the kitchen was empty
'It's clear' I said — Sandy and me headed out bare butt. ALL'A SUDDEN A BLAST 'rupted out the right side'a the hall. Francis yip-yelled who batted on a pot, Wilbur whistled holdin water glasses to his eyes like binoc'lars. Heather hooted and clapped hands as the cacklin crew follered us up the hall. Bors' head popped out his door, Bors' eyeballs popped out his head. Smilin Sandy and me tossed a wave — reared right into Sandy's room and slammed the door on the cacklin crew. Both of us roared, another secret mission tucked under our belts

After we all was sittin in the control room with a b'lloon floatin from the chairs. Heard famil'yur wheezy sounds from atop the steps. We swung round, and there was six bloody aliens. As Bors swung, his ci-gar hit Francis' b'lloon — burst it!
'Oops!' I went, with all of us startled
The aliens chattered. Suddenly one grabbed a

piece'a prickly cactus from a plant b'side, hurled it to Sandy's b'lloon, bustin it

Aliens jabbered 'citedly, pointed, then stormed down the stairs. I grabbed Flower Butt off the counter — held him in front and the aliens stepped back

We headed away from 'em, t'ward the stairs — raced up the hall to the storage room and locked the door

We stood and waited

Could hear 'poofs' in the control room — the aliens burst th'other b'lloons

Then the engines started up

The ship changed direction

After awhile the engines was off

Wilbur looked at his watch

'Been a couple of hours'

'Don't hear nothin' I said

'I wonder if they've gone?' said Sandy low

'Yeah, to have their lunch or afternoon sex or somthn' I said

'Probably afternoon sex' said Francis

We peaked our heads out

I went first holdin Flower Butt forward, follered by the others — to the top'a the control room steps

'They're gone!' I said

'They'll be back' said Sandy nervous

We headed for snacks in the kitchen, then back to

the control room. Wilbur fired the engines, and turned the ship's direction. He asked

'Boris, you were saying your specialty is . . . ?'

'Solar hoolography. Use hoolograms combined vit Sun rays — make heat, light, power generate'

'Hum . . .' I looked round impressed

'Unlimited energy from Sun. All need is to harness'

'Oh' went Sandy

'Halso make hoolograms for high performance hair-craft'

'You can make holograms?' asked Heather

'Yaw. Make pictures in air — not real but look real'

'I saw holograms in a mall once' said Sandy

'So did I' added Heather

'They're cool'

'How do you make holograms?' asked Heather

'Vel, use lasers, but can do vit compooter. Compooter-generated hoolographic image possible'

'The aliens are afraid of the skunk' said Heather

'Yaw'

'Boris, can you make a skunk hologram?' asked Heather

'A big one . . . fill the ship' I added

'Vel . . . '

'Boris, you can try' said Francis 'I'll help with the computer calculations'

'Yaw, let's do!'

The guys hi-fived

So's Flower Butt stood on a glass plate — Francis

photographed him with his phone from b'low, top, all sides, ever which way

'Ve put stick into compooter, get images from all sides'

Bors worked at his compooter — Ha ha! With Francis, his right-hand man . . . . . Ah-ha ha

'Compooter hoologram produce wavefronts vit any prescribed amplitude and phase distribution'

'Right' Francis said. He looked to us — made a face

'Very basic' said Bors

'Sure is' said Francis, who looked to us, shrugged his shoulders

'Color information hoologram is encoded in spatial frequencies of carrier fringes'

Francis nodded. So did us all. Didn't have a clue

'Francees, you hold steady XY contingents, I manipulate images'

'Right'

Later Bors positioned this box

'Ve aim shutter'

Suddenly a beam'a colored light shot out'a the box, and a SIX-FOOTS OSTRICH WAS STANDIN IN THE ROOM

We looked at one 'nother

'Vrong — vrong!'

'WOW!' went Sandy

Bors worked s'more at his compooter, the ostrich shrunk

'Ve get right!'

Them sumbitch yeller-greens decided to prance up the hall 'gain. Was gettin tired of 'em
'They're here!' I 'sclaimed
Bors worked quick — all a sudden a TEN FOOTS SKUNK APPEARED IN THE CONTROL ROOM
The aliens freaked — dashed this way and that squealin, some bumped to the floor. They run up the hall — into the spacesuits room and slammed the door
We could see the ship outside door open again on a compooter screen
'Francis, close the door' said Wilbur
Francis nodded, typed and the door swung closed

We looked round, and could see the brown and yeller ship cruisin near us
'Boris, can you make the skunk bigger?' asked Heather
'Yaw, I tink'
'Can . . . can ya keep makin it bigger so's it surrounds our rocket?' I asked
'Freak'em' said Sandy
'I try'
Bors set to work — 'ventually throwed his thumb in the air
The skunk growed BIGGER — BIGGER, kep gettin so big it filled the room. Then went THROUGH THE WALLS

In our compooters we could see on the external cam'ras the skunk image surroundin the ship — so we was this BIG, HUGE BLACK 'N WHITE STRIPED SKUNK STREAMIN THROUGH SPACE!

The alien ship follerin us stopped, did a 'mediate lift-up and streaked into the stars

We all hopped up and hi-fived

Wilbur soon fired the engines and ole Spaceship Faithful shot forward. Then he said

'Bet we won't see them again!'

'I hope not' said Sandy

'Wonder if they blew our artificial gravity?' I asked

'Could be' said Wilbur

'They'll never believe this back home' said Heather

'I tell' said Bors

'So will I . . . But they'll say we're hallucinating' added Heather

'I take peecture'

'DID YOU?' went Wilbur

On Bors' compooter screen 'peared the ten foots skunk, the aliens all freakin behind it!

'Holy shy . . . we got a snap' I 'sclaimed

'Lots'

Bors flashed a couple more on the screen

'Great work, Bo-Bo!' 'sclaimed Francis, hi-fivin Bors

Later we all sat on the carpet sippin tea

'Pork'pines — check this' I said, lookin in m'book

'the male rises on his hind legs, so does the female, the guy pees all over her from head to foots, then they have wild, pee-filled sex. Cool, huh?'
'Robin pees all over me before we do it'
'All'a time' I patted Sandy's arm
'Doesn't it get messy? I mean the bed' asked Heather
'I pee on her in the shower'
Sandy nodded 'How we do it'
'Yikes! I'll have to try it' 'sclaimed Francis

We sat awhile. Wilbur said
'Well it's been quite a day'
'You two sure started it off with a bang' said Heather
'In more ways than one' I said. Sandy chuckled — hit m'arm
'Pee-filled?' asked Heather
'Not this time' I said

'You can be sure we'll wear our clothes tomorrow' said Sandy
'Oh why! I think you both look very handsome without clothes' replied Heather
'Een old country alvays svim bare'
'Oh so do I, whenever I get the chance' said Francis
'Feel free' added Wilbur

'So why don't we?' asked Heather
'Swim bare?' asked Wilbur

'Silly . . . walk around without clothes'

   Everyone held our cups, looked at Heather

'Kidding of course' said Wilbur

'Why not? It's the most natural thing. And we know each other well enough by now'

'HERE!?' went Francis

'Sure'

'Ha ha' I laughed

'Robin?' asked Heather

'OK'

'One, Sandy?'

'Here?'

'Oh-h . . . . Boris?'

'Vel . . . '

'Got two, Wilbur?'

'I'm the captain'

'So'

'Try anything once' he said

'Ha ha, three, Francis?'

'All of them?'

'If hevryone, hi'

'A majority, Sandy?'

'OK'

'Ha ha' I laughed

'C'mon Francis' said Heather

'HERE?'

'Oh-h-h . . . '

All of us looked at Francis, who threw up his hands. We laughed and sat glancin round

'So do I have to be first? . . . Chickens' said Heather

'NO, ROBIN WILL!'

'Sandy!'

I pinched her

'OW!'

'OK, on the count of three' continued Heather

'THOUSAND' innerjected Francis

'Aliens watchin?' I asked

'They're gone' Heather said

'Hold on, on three, or on *go* after three?' asked Francis

'On three'

'One' she continued

'Hold on -- ' went Francis

'ONE . . . Two . . . Three . . . '

Heather started to unbutton her blouse. Sandy giggled, slipped off her T-shirt. All of us tugged off trousers, shorts and all. We sat bare gigglin, toastin tea cups in the Sun

White mist floats over a stage, big puffy orange clouds cruise by — Sandy and me drift in aboard a orange cloud, wearin white robes strummin harps with green leaf wreaths round our heads. A pile'a soft yeller butterflies fluttered t'ward us, millions'a yeller and white butterflies come swoopin over our heads as both of us ducked. I looked over to Sandy, smiled and plucked the harp. A couple'a big beaver chawed on a tree in the distance, the beavers workin busy as ALL A SUDDEN this pile'a white rabbits hopped t'ward us from off in the distance, dozens and hunderds'a white and pink and green rabbits hoppin faster, comin closer. Sandy and me ducked as the hares hopped over our heads and was lost in the fog

'WOW' I went, plucked the harp and started to sing

Pluck

'Of Sandy, Sweet Sandy, this song shall be sung

A whole pile of Wonders all rolled into one
Pluck

Of wisdoms so many, Of years Oh so young

Bright eyes so beautiful, Cheeks oh so rosy

And honey color freckles speckled on her fair nosey

That's Sandy, Oh Sandy, sweet child of the Sun

A whole batch of beauties, all rolled in to o ne'
Pluck

'Oh Robin . . . that was so-o beautiful'

'Thanks Sandy'

'Look Robin, the clouds are getting brighter'

'So they are. The orange ones are turnin yeller'

'And white whiter'

'U-huh'

'Robin, it's so awesome'

126

'Gloryous Sandy'
'Oh Robin'
'Oh Sandy'
'Oh ROBIN'
'Oh SANDY'
'Robin, wake up Robin'
'OH . . . . Sandy!'

I woke up and propped on a elbow, watched Sandy who leaned forward bare 'cept for a apron
'Up Robin, we're preparing for the feast'
'Oh . . . K'

I rised, headed to the kitchen, and joined all per-parin for our landin feast, everyone bare wearin aprons, and talk 'bout a pile'a pots, pans and pinchin

Steam floats up from plates and bowls spread b'low the rubber plant in center'a the control room. Some of the crew took off our aprons and sat on cushions. We had Heather's l'il samwiches fixed fancy with pickles, olives and toothpicks. Wilbur's corns on the cob and Francis' 'scarguts and red crabs apples, Bors' rhubarbs pie we passed on 'cept Bors, Sandy's peach ice cream and m'huckleberry pancakes and corn grits

The external cam'ras showed on the monitors half the black 'n white skunk hoologram was faded. In front the Earth was so big, lit up by the Sun on right

'The Sun is so bright' said Sandy. I looked in the book 'Our Sun orbits 'nother Sun. True or false?'

'True' said Bors

'Does it?' asked Heather

'Question. Will the Sun, when it finally explodes' asked Francis 'Shrink down to a white dwarf star, or implode to a black hole . . . Class?'

I put up m'hand

'Yes?'

'Teacher, I don't care'

'Go stand in the corner. Anyone more intellectual here?'

Bors put up his hand

'Me'

'Anyone?' asked Francis

'Boris' said Sandy

'I'm talking about humans'

'OK, I'll volunteer. I like dwarfs' Sandy said

'Dopey's m'favorite' I added

'Figures' went Heather

'Hey!'

   I throwed a roll at her

'OK, stupids! Teacher will come to the rescue' said Francis

'Oh good!' went Sandy

'Dwarf' said Francis

'Vite dwarf. I know'

'Nothing. You know nothing. How can an object with no brain capacity *know*?'

'OK folks' said Heather

'That's Wilbur's line' I said

'Boris saved us with the hologram' said Sandy

'Big brain' I nods to Bors

'A fluke' went Francis

   I had m'Facts book in m'lap

'When a drone honeybee does it with a queen –– '

'He goes yippee!' cut in Francis

'Nope . . . his balls explode and the poor dude falls dead'

'What a way to go' said Wilbur

''Cordin to this survey' I continued 'Women would rather have money than sex'

'How much money?' asked Sandy

'How much sex?' and Francis

'Lots — I guess' I said

'I take chocolate' said Bors. Everone looked at him 'I like chocolate better'

He popped a square in his mouth

'Sure, fat boy' said Francis

'Cvreep'

'FOLKS!' went Wilbur

After all of us toasted and clicked our cups

'Let's have a toast, to the most . . . the best . . . most wonderful crew ever to fly through space' said Sandy

'Here Here' Clink went Heather

'To Sandy' I said

Clink

'And Robin' Clink Clink

'To Heather, Oh social guru' toasted Wilbur

'And Wilbur, Super Space Captain' toasted Heather

Clink Clink

'To Boris, oh great space scientist' said Wilbur

'And cute, yaw?'

We all laughed

'To Francis, oh horny one' I toasted

Clink Clink

All of us sipped tea, smilin happy

Next mornin we hopped in our seats excited again 'cause the planet had grown so huge in front, with green forests and jungles seen clear, blue rivers winded round, white capped rock mountains zoomed into the sky — all of us watched mesm'rized. Suddenly purple and yeller suction cups come claspin onto the spaceship windows, long skinny purple arms wrapped round and round the ship as we slammed out of our seats, bounced off the walls . . . Wilbur hollered to all stay POSITIVE and think of somthn . . . the purple octo . . . ho ho . . . the octopus AH HA HA, only kiddin, ha ha. Well the octo . . . Ho ho — no really, our spaceship speeded fast and Wilbur fired the engines for slowin us

'We're in the planet's gravity grip' he hollered

We sat erect and was pressed down in our seats. Then the ship went shootin in orbit with engines off, we checked it thorough for landin. Wilbur started knittin. He waved the sweater in the air. One side was lots bigger than the other

'Cool, huh?'

'It's awesome' Sandy looked at me, held back a laugh

'Laugh Sandy' said Wilbur 'You'll suffer for it one day'

Sandy stopped grinnin as I held back m'laugh. Wilbur looked at me. I shrugged

'What I'll do is knit the whole sweater, cut it in half, then knit halves to fit both sides . . . and knit them together'

'I don't think that's how it's normally done' said Heather

'I'm a trailblazer'

'Makes sense' I said

Some of us watched the scenery through b'noc'lars, our minds blown by what we saw. Y'know, this planet is so awesome beautiful — too bad we hafta leave it. Y'know, maybe we don't. Like, things'll clean up somehow. Hope so

'What's the Earth's estimated weight?' asked Francis

'Who knows?' commented Bors

'I do' said Francis

'Six thousand pounds' I guessed

'What an idiot'

'Robin, he called you an idiot' said Sandy
'So'
'Aren't you —— ' she started
'Sandy, some people . . . doesn't fizz me'
'OK, stupids, the planet's estimated weight is six sex-
tillion tons' he said
'Vy sex?'
' — Tillion'
'Why not sixtillion tons?' I wondered
'Sex is more —— ' started Francis
'Sexy' said Heather
'Right. And there's a lot of it going on this planet, so it
rests at sextillion' he said
'You making this up?' asked Wilbur
'It's in the book'
    Francis showed the book
'Still doesn't tell you anything. I mean, like, who knows
what a sextillion is?' questioned Sandy smartly
'It's a multiple of millions . . . I guess' answered Francis

    Later Wilbur said
'You know, astronauts often become alcoholics'
'Oh?' went Heather
'What's experienced in space is so profound, being
back on Earth becomes anti-climactic'
'Sort of a come down' said Sandy
'Right. So let's —— '
'Not b'come alco'lics'

'I already am' said Sandy

'No y'aren't' I tickled her. Then pointed

'Look, there's the Am'zon river'

'It's so big' Sandy said

'World's super river' said Wilbur

'Longest in the world' added Francis. Heather said

'Nile is'

'Lot you know'

'I'd love to go there sometime' Sandy said

'Am'zon's a blast' I went

'Oh look — three rainbows' pointed Heather

'Wow!' went Sandy

The Sun dropped b'low the horizon behind as we clipped to the night side. Cities sparked all around and stars overhead

'There's Vegas' Francis said

'Lit up like a alien landin strip' I added. Sandy said

'Don't mention aliens'

'Right'

'Sure looks like something from outer space' said Francis

The strip'a blue horizon in front growed brighter, the Sun popped up sprayin yeller rays all over as we clipped 'cross the day side, over trop'cal islands sparklin in the em'rald blue and millions'a white geese cruisin cross a green plain — all of us comin excited 'cause it looked so awesome. Francis hopped to the piano and made up a song

Plunk Plunk

'Sing a Song a Hi a Ho . . . of a planet we love and know

of fields of green and seas of blue

islands and forests and rivers too

Plunk

. . . of rainbows shining in the sky'

'Of itchy squiters'

I sang

and parking meters'

'Ha ha . . .

he went

'Woof woof' barked Wilbur

'Of white wooly sheep'

sang Sandy

'Ha ha' Plunk

'And billy goats going beep' and Heather

'Of barking dogs' Wilbur

'and fat ole' hogs' Heather 'gain

'Yessir' went Francis

'Beeg bull frogs oond leetle polly vogs'

We laughed

'HA HA' Plunk Plunk

'I don't understand it, Jack' come a voice over the speakers 'Sounds like singing'

Ripple Plunk

'Yes, and piano playing. Let's see if we can make contact. SPACESHIP FAITHFUL, SPACESHIP FAITHFUL, is that you? . . . Over'

All of us looked to one other. Wilbur grabbed the mikerphone

'WOOF' he barked, crackin us to pieces

'WOOF-WOOF'

We slapped our knees

'He's barking, Bill. He just barked at us'

'Wooof'

Everyone roared

'There's laughter, Bill. Spaceship Faithful, is that you barking?'

'Woof, sure is'

'HE SAID IT IS, BILL. THIS IS JACK. ARE YOU OK?'

'We're perfect'

'THEY'RE PERFECT, BILL. HE SAID THEY'RE PERFECT!'

'Couldn't be better'

'Well I'L-L-L BE, we had you for gonners'

'We're fine'

'Well GOL-L-Y-Y!'

Wilbur and Jack started chattin excited, the rest of us watched the scenery and talked to OFPM folk. On our external cam'ras two-thirds'a the skunk was gone — some black 'n white stripes still run 'long the outside

After we cleaned up the ship for landin, 'cause ya wanna make a good impression, Ha ha!

The spaceship started lowerin, it bashed through white clouds with the engines roarin, out into the Sun again we clipped over blue ocean, with white icebergs floatin round, oer green forests and gold desserts and forests s'more, 'cross cotton fields comin to a blue sparklin sea on the horizon and beach beside towerin palms trees. We spotted a yeller square launch pad beside the OFPM buildin, all of us glancin down seein crowds and hellycopters circlin. We looked to each other and shrugged. Wilbur gripped the steerer, flipped a lever, our heads whipped back in our seats as the spaceship shot out over the water, away from the waitin buildin. We laughed, knowin had to do her — Wilbur spinned it round again and aimed the ship toward the OFPM square, we circled the area

'Gotta do this right' Wilbur hollered as he threw up

his thumb. The spaceship lowered t'ward the pad — we bounced up down up. Finally landed. We sat dazed. Heather clutched her side
'Third landing' smiled Wilbur

Legs come out the bottom sides of the ship, pushin us erect

We all sat watchin palms trees swayin in the windows overhead, beside blue and white waves that rolled in on the beach which raced into the sky
'Woah!' said Heather
'I'm just agog' said Francis
'You're a hog?' I asked
'Agog, silly'
'What's a gog?' asked Sandy
'Sounds like something to do with a dog' added Heather
'Egg nog' went Sandy
'Agog with delight, stupids'
'Whataya say we take this one *real easy*' s'ggested Wilbur. Francis asked
'Tea anyone?'

We nodded, headed into the kitchen where we sat nibblin cookies, drippin tea in our laps
'Must be a million people out there' 'sclaimed Wilbur
'Give or take a hundred thousand' added Heather
'Press, TV cameras'
'A-yup' I went

'Who's for showing them where we're at?' he asked

'I guess we'll have to eventually' said Heather

'I mean, go out there . . . . as we are'

All jaws dropped, we looked at Wilbur 'stonished

'Of course you're kidding' said Heather

'He's kidding' Francis smiled, nodded

'C'mon. Be a once in a lifetime thing. They'll never forget us'

'You're daft!' said Heather

'We'll go down in history . . . Robin?'

'We-l-l-l . . . my gramma's watchin'

'Sandy?'

'OK' she laughed

'I ain't no chicken' I said

Sandy and me hi-fived

'Three, Francis?'

'OUT THERE!'

He covered hisself with his hand

'Boris?'

'Vel . . . '

'TRY ANYTHING ONCE!' 'sclaimed Francis. We laughed, then Bors said

'If everyone, hi'

'FIVE, a majority' went Wilbur

'YOU ARE ALL CRAZY! YOU'VE LOST IT! You're kidding of course!'

Heather looked round

'C'mon Heather' I said

'I'M NOT STEPPING OUT OF HERE WITHOUT EVERY STITCH OF MY CLOTHING'

Nobody moved. After awhile Wilbur said
'Gentlemen, lady . . . '

He rised followed by us all, 'cept Heather who clutched the edge'a the table. Wilbur come up behind her, placed his hands under Heather's elbows, nodded to us as we lifted Heather. Sandy opened the door — Heather stretched her legs forward tryin to hold back who we carried into the hall. She squirmed as we passed her room and clothes waitin folded neat on the bed. I grabbed Flower Butt out'a m'bedroom. We stepped into the spacesuits room and compression chamber, Heather held solid in Wilbur's iron grip. Buzzed open the door, and heard
'Seventh floor, ladies' bathroom -- '

We banged the button. Poked our heads out the oval hatch — felt a blast'a fresh ocean air float in the ship, and Sun direct on our bare bodies so soothin. We spotted the couple'a OFPM workers tryin to push the el'vator 'cross the launch pad — it 'peared stuck. We waved, hollered all was OK and tossed out the rope ladder
'WELL, HERE GOES' said Wilbur

We stepped out on the yeller rungs one by one, Wilbur eased Heather out with us helpin, pryin her fingers off from around the door, we climbed down the rope rungs. I carried Flower Butt. Stepped onto the hot ce-ment launch pad, and stood shieldin our eyes, watchin the white OFPM buildin and people millin about. News hellycopters flew over us. Sandy started hiccupin so I patted her back

'And a one, and a two' said Wilbur

We looked to each other, shrugged and started forward holdin hands, chucklin. Flower Butt waddled behind. We strolled past the el'vator operators whose eyeballs was poppin. Tossed 'em waves and continued 'long. And maybe it was 'cause the ce-ment was so hot to our foots, or maybe bein just so galdarn excited over the situation and all, but suddenly we shot up our arms round the shoulders of the ones beside us, kicked our heels up in the air, and formed a chorus line'a gigglin naked loonies dancin and laughin 'cross the launch pad t'ward the waitin buildin and crowds all around

We approached the open glass doors'a the buildin surrounded by people — eyeballs popped, folks cheered and laughed and slapped knees. Lots'a news mikerphones, everyone patted our backs as we squeezed into the crowded room. Cam'ra flashes popped round us

POP   POP   POP

Wilbur waved at a cam'ra

'HI MOM!'

Jack and Bill was there

'You made it back!' Jack 'sclaimed, givin me a big hug.
Did same to everyone

'Yessir!' I grinned

'What happened to your clothes?' asked Bill

'Figured we'd exit the spaceship casual' said Sandy

'Did you ever!' this lady 'sclaimed

'The spaceship has black and white stripes?' Jack asked

'How's that?'

'It's a long story' answered Wilbur

'You'll never believe us' Heather said

    All the crew roared. We stood in a circle facin out,
hurlin back the answers

We was tested for two weeks. They wanted to make
sure we hadn't picked up outer space bugs in our
brains or somthn. One day in a corridor I chatted with
Jack and Bill

'The fact you made it back is the main thing' said Jack

'Yeah'

'As far as should we evacuate the whole planet — well
if you guys are an example –– ' started Bill

'MAYBE WE SHOULDN'T!' innerjected Jack. Bill laughed
and said

'We'll have to think about it'

'Do we get our bonuses?' I asked

'Yes'

Sandy, Heather and me was watchin a TV in the rec

room. News was talkin 'bout us bein lost in space, then the 'nouncer said

' . . . and aside from engine malfunctions on the lost OFPM spaceflight, nothing out of the ordinary happened'

I roared, clapped hands — Heather, Sandy, all us had a good laugh. And y'know, they kept a lid on it like that. As I said, this's the *real deal* story

Well time come on the yeller launch pad when the spacecrew waved and hugged, then Heather, Wilbur, Bors and Francis boarded a small OFPM plane. Sandy and me was offered to stay 'nother week and we accepted. Both of us held hands and waved as the plane sped 'cross the launch pad, lifted up into the blue sky and headed north

It kicked off the next weeks Sandy and me got to know one n'other s'more, with both of us strollin hand in hand up sunset-lit beaches, the wet sand comin shiny orange like glass as we strolled barefoots leavin our footprints behind — kissin under the white full Moon and star-filled skies. Both of us arrived at a conclusion, decided to spend a spell with one 'nother

So the day come when Sandy and I said our farewellin to the OFPM folk, who'd become real good friends, and we got lots'a bucks for sellin our stories.

So we packed our backpacks and Flower Butt, me and Sandy headed to the airport

I strolled to the ticket counter where a lady, 'bout 18, asked

'Your name?'

'Robin Rooster'

Her jaw dropped — eyes popped. She stood gawkin, her hands to her cheeks

'YOU MEAN THEE ROBIN ROOSTER?'

I nodded. The girl give out a shriek, then fell to the floor. Other airport folk rushed over and helped her up. The girls eyes opened, looked at me and conked out again. The airport folk fanned her face, pointed at me and Sandy. Words spread and a crowd come round, squeezin closer. Some ladies shrieked, hollered ROBIN, held out pads for us to sign — we posed for pitures. It got real crowded, so Sandy and me squeezed toward the airport door draggin Flower Butt in his cage, out into the sunshine as ALL A SUDDEN screamin chicks, callin m'name, come runnin. I raced for the waitin plane and flew up the steps. Some teenage girls tried to climb, and was knocked down by airport security guys as I stood on top'a the steps wavin

I tossed a kiss or two, and asked security fellers if they could fetch Flower Butt, who did. Both of us headed into the plane, strollin by admirin passengers.

Found m'seat beside Sandy already there, who had it more easy

The plane rised into the sky — Sandy and me stretched our necks, spotted the OFPM buildin and spaceship in center'a the yeller launch pad

We flew north to Sandy's home town, said hello and bye to folk, and then headed west a bit

o   o   o

Plans often change when ya meet a female, huh?

I was gon' construct a sailboat and float over the planet. But with the bread we got for our stories, Sandy and me decided to build us a log cabin here in the mountains. With Flower Butt we're livin beside a lake in a big white tent havin a yeller butterly on front with blue eyes that Sandy sewed. Strollin 'bout bare breathin the clean country air, growin a garden and sproutin lots, sunflower seeds and white ses'mes and eatin wild greens and pickin berries, and we're thinkin'a gettin a goat and some bees. Maybe chickens for eggs. And we heard from Heather and Wilbur together on the west coast, and Francis and Bors are back in Zoo City, and we're all thinkin'a havin a big reunion sometimes in the future

Well it's time to say so long for now, and get back to hammerin and sawin and scrapin. Never worked so hard in m'life. There's somthn pure 'bout it though, somthn simple, somthn right. Ho ho, stopt Sandy . . . Hee hee, lego!

A flock'a honkin white swans is flyin over in the blue sky formin a perfec V lit gold by the sun. Well so long for now, and Sandy's hollered to say goodbye, so so long for Sandy, and so long for now

REPORTER 'So that's it Robin, the story'

ROBIN 'That's her honey, for now anyhow'

Robin Sun hails from Montreal, Canada. He headed to Vancouver after university, then lived in the Arctic and later the Yukon mountains with the bears and gophers. Toronto followed, then California where he resides with his turtle, Speed Freak. He has been a Hollywood actor, wilderness road surveyor, recruiting agent, advertising executive, taxi driver, carpenter and waiter at Beverly Hills hotels and the Oscars.

To receive free newsletter
or
Robin Rooster blogs
go to
robinsun.ca

72780479R00090

Made in the USA
Columbia, SC
27 June 2017